THE LIGHTHOUSE

JACOB BILLINGS

PUBLISHED BY FASTPENCIL PUBLISHING

D1261669

First Edition

http://fp.fastpencil.com

Printed in the United States of America

TABLE OF CONTENTS

Nightmare 7

Arrival 15

White House on a Hill 23

The Shores 31

The Lighthouse 39

Forbidden 49

Stealing Away 59

The Legend of the Silver Pearl 69

Up the Trellis 77

Deep Sea 85

The Locket 93

The Letter..101

Gone 109

The Forgotten Portrait.................................... 123

The Map..129

The Creaky Stair 135

The Jewelry Box.. 143

The Globe 151

The Telescope 157

The Secret of the Lighthouse..........................165

Darkness 169

The Storm..177

Missing 185

The Search 191

Message in a Bottle 199

Charlotte...209

Remembering 217

The Forgotten Cove..223

Shipwreck...229

The Grotto 233

Fading Away 239

Hard to Starboard 245

The Light of the Lighthouse 251

To those in my life who

have always been a light...

&

NIGHTMARE

The rumble of the car wheels was faint, but constant. Grace listened as her mom and dad spoke in happy tones. Dad got a raise on his job, so that meant a lot of good things.

"You know, we should take a vacation sometime. Get away from the busy, New York streets for a while," Mom suggested.

Dad evaluated, "We could, but then again, I don't want to lose the job."

They both laughed.

"Where would we go?" Dad asked.

Mom was imaginative, "We could go somewhere in the country... maybe down by the beach. Don't you have a relative down there, somewhere?"

"A great aunt," Dad said. "I've never met her, though."

"Didn't you tell me that she is a strange person, one who mostly keeps to herself?" Mom asked.

Dad paused for a moment, obviously deep in thought. His aunt was such a distant memory, one who he didn't often consider, and so now he silently reflected.

Grace wished he would have said more, and suddenly, she was begging him to say more. "Dad, what is it..."

The dream began to stretch and blur. Grace knew the dream. It was the nightmare she always had. She wanted to scream, but she couldn't. And though she tried to kick and make any sort of noise, she was paralyzed.

Then she felt as if it was all being pulled farther and farther away. In the darkness of her mind, she heard the car crash once and then again. Without warning, she was spinning, tumbling end over end.

Finally she broke through the paralysis and screamed, "Dad! Mom!"

But there was no answer. There never was an answer.

It was a bolt of lightning that suddenly awoke her from the dream. She sat up, feeling stiff and tense. Breathing hard, she shivered in the cold sweat that she always woke up with, as the same, heavy darkness filled the room.

She lay back on her bed, still breathing hard. Grace wondered how she would ever make it through the night. At first she wanted to stay awake, but memories of her parents and the car crash came flooding into her mind. Then she wished that she could fall back asleep so that time would pass more quickly.

But sleep was coming slowly. Grace lay quietly and focused on the rhythmic rocking of the boat. The motion reminded her of a rocking chair. It was peaceful, but after a time, it became a little annoying.

The constant creaking of the cabin she was in helped her remember how many hundreds of feet of water were beneath her. She bristled and turned her thoughts elsewhere.

Her father's silence, when it came to his great aunt, scared Grace. It seemed as if there was a long lost secret about her. And really, it wouldn't have mattered much, except for the fact that this great aunt was now her closest living relative. After the death of her parents, Grace's great aunt had adopted her–the letter of agreement was tucked safely in her suitcase.

Closing her eyes, Grace let her mind drift over the events of the past month. It started with the car accident. A semi's brakes had malfunctioned, as it was about to merge into the tide of cars on the freeway. The giant truck had rolled forward, out of control, and hit her family's car in the side with such force that it sent the car spinning. As they spun, the car behind theirs didn't have time to react, so it had hit the other side of the car. The impact of the second crash sent their car rolling off of the road.

Grace had blacked out there...

And from that moment on, nothing was the same. Her whole world had changed.

Social Workers took her off to an orphanage of sorts, explaining that it was only a temporary home until they got things figured out.

Instead of a home, however, Grace had felt trapped like a prisoner. It seemed like she had spent years in that jail, and she had never felt so alone in her life. When the letter finally came announcing that her great aunt had been found and would adopt her,

Grace was filled with hope that she would never have to feel so alone again.

Grace had taken the flight from New York to Philadelphia only a couple days before. In Philadelphia, she boarded an ocean liner that would take her to the Mackinac Island. There was no public airliner that flew to the island, so the only access to the island was by boat. It wasn't a long journey, but it had seemed like forever to Grace, as she anticipated meeting her great aunt. The ocean was infinite in its ever-moving tides. She had stood on the dock, watching the waves for hours.

Then night had come, and she had fallen asleep in her cabin, only to awake from the nightmare. Her racing thoughts seemed to fill up the small, cabin room. Grace was never one to be claustrophobic, but the room seemed to somehow trap in her fears and her thoughts. At last, she climbed off the bed, and stealing the coverlet, she wrapped herself up and made her way to the exit.

The door had a small, round window in it. Grace peeped through for a moment. Everything appeared dark. She opened the door as quietly as she could, but it still creaked softly on its hinges.

Outside, the smell of the ocean greeted her. The scent of rain lingered, though no droplets fell. Grace could still feel the moisture in the air, and a cool wind played with her hair. As her eyes adjusted to the darkness, she could see the ghostly tide crashing against the side of the boat, as traces of foam rode the waves. The boat's stern cut the water like a knife, sending ripples receding from its sides.

Above, the clouds from the storm were thick, but all at once an opening had formed in the clouds, and through that opening, stars shone down like diamonds in the night. Grace gasped at the sight. Being one who had lived in the city all her life, she had never seen the stars like this. In fact, she had never known there were so many of them. Here in the darkness, away from the city lights, the sky was endless. As she watched, the clouds became more and more sparse, and the stars sprinkled the endlessness of sky with twinkling lights.

For a long time, she just stood and gazed up at the stars, believing that somehow her mom and her dad were watching over her. The stars brought her a comfort – a promise that everything would be all right.

Then a splash from below caught her attention. Startled, she looked down into the water. There was another splash, then another. It took several splashes before she was able to catch sight of something glimmering in the water – dolphins.

They swam neck in neck with the boat, seeming to be in the middle of a race at its best. They dove in and out of the water. It almost seemed to Grace that they were showing off to her, trilling and clicking as they jumped out of the water, then falling back in with barely a splash.

Grace yawned. She was still tired. The dolphins, wind, and stars had helped her forget the past for a time and filled her with peace. She turned, ready to return to her cabin when she saw a light on the shore in the distance.

She stared at it through the fog, wondering what it was. Then, like a breath of fresh air, she realized – it was a lighthouse!

The lighthouse stood guard, watching over her like a loving parent, like her mom and dad always had and always would. The lighthouse was there to guide her and lead her in the right direction.

And now, although she stood there on the ocean liner feeling more confused and insecure than she'd ever felt in all her life, Grace knew that she was headed in the right direction.

Closing the cabin door behind her, Grace smiled for the first time since the car accident.

She knew that this island, with her aunt and the lighthouse, held a new life for her. But somehow it seemed that somewhere in it all, a secret lurked. Grace recognized the presence of it. She loved secrets, and in her mind she could sense when there was a secret for her to unravel. She knew that there was something she was meant to do on the island. The glow from the lighthouse felt like the greeting of an old friend. It was as if it knew her and hadn't seen her for centuries, but now that she was finally returning, was relieved to see her again.

Grace laughed at herself. How strange to feel a relationship with a lighthouse, especially one she'd never seen it before, but she knew the feeling, the feeling of connection... Was it the lighthouse that held the mystery? Or was it her great aunt and the distance she kept from everyone? Grace knew that where there were questions, there had to be answers, and somehow, deep within her, she knew that she would find the answers, whatever they were.

Grace climbed on the bed and lay back on the pillow. Now the darkness of her mind was filled with dreams of her new home. Her sole desire in the days preceding this one had been to find home. It had become so strongly rooted in her heart that she rarely thought of anything else. In the quiet, Grace prayed, as she had hundreds of times before, that her great aunt would accept her – that her great aunt would become more than just a legal guardian – that she would be a real friend for her hungry soul.

With peaceful thoughts and faith that she was on her way home, Grace fell asleep to the gentle moaning of the boat as it rose and fell on the ocean tides.

ARRIVAL

It was the very same morning, only a couple hours later, when Sam stood in the Main Gallery, just beneath the Watch of the very same lighthouse Grace had seen from the ocean liner.

He was often up at the crack of dawn so that he could watch the boats as they came into the port.

Sam was tall for his sixteen-years, with sandy, unkempt, blond hair and shining, blue eyes. He lived in the lighthouse with his uncle. It had been this way for as long as he could remember.

The morning was a cold one for July, and Sam, with his binoculars, was scanning the horizon for boats. In the distance, through the fog of the morning, he could make out the ocean liner as it materialized in the fog. Dropping his binoculars so they hung around his neck, he climbed down through the hatch to the long, spiral staircase.

Racing down the stairs, he hardly noticed the step that squeaked louder than the rest. Sometimes he'd try to be careful so that he wouldn't wake his uncle, and he avoided the step completely, but this morning he didn't care.

Within moments, Sam had cleared the staircase and had rushed through the front door of the lighthouse. Picking up speed, he dashed along the beach.

Sam loved to run. Whenever things were hard or he needed a break, he'd run. Sometimes he would run just for the sheer pleasure of it. He loved the feeling of the wind against his face and the ground rushing beneath him. But best of all, he loved running along the beach. When the sun was rising, the sky lit up in brilliant colors, and the water sparkled. He loved to feel the sand squish beneath his bare feet. And when the tide came in, he liked the way it tried to pull the sand out from underneath him, but he was too fast for it. Sometimes the tide would cascade up around him, and he'd get drenched, but Sam never cared.

The port was only a couple miles away, and he had cleared the distance many times. For Sam, the run was almost effortless.

...

Morning light streamed in through the little, round window in Grace's cabin room on the ocean liner, and when she looked out the window, she was reassured to see the island growing in the distance. The rocky cliffs and sandy beaches greeted her. In the morning light, she could see the lighthouse standing to greet her. It was a tall lighthouse, painted mostly white, except for the roofs and gables that were a dark grey.

She stepped outside the door. Standing on the deck, Grace watched as the liner moved into the pier. Seagulls flew to and fro, singing the song of the ocean as they went.

It was a beautiful morning, not too hot and not too cold – Grace noted pleasantly. She also noticed that the storm clouds, from the night before, had completely vanished.

The island looked simple enough, perhaps more of a country-styled place, very different from the busy streets she had left behind. As she looked at the old-fashioned village, it almost seemed to Grace as if she had boarded a boat that had transported her back in time.

Little fishing boats, some with powered motors, and some with sails, lined the pier. Fishermen pulled in nets or raised their sails. It was a busy sight.

Soon the ocean liner reached the dock, and steps were set up for the passengers to exit. Grace picked up her black suitcase and followed the slow traffic as it made its way off of the boat.

Sam arrived at the dock just as the passengers began to leave. He made his way up the opposite direction, weaving through the crowd. He accidentally bumped into Grace, apologizing without stopping. He was looking for the captain, too eager for extra apologies.

The captain of the ocean liner was pacing the deck, both of his hands behind his back in pride. He looked at his watch and smiled again. The ship had arrived precisely when it was supposed to. The captain preferred to be on time. In fact it was his aspiration to do exactly this, but if he could, he never minded being a few moments early. He believed in things that were predictable. A few minutes late to the port could mean a few more minutes late leaving the port, and then he would never be able to make up for the lost time, so the captain always stayed right on schedule.

According to schedule, right about now he expected Sam to arrive – the boy from the lighthouse.

"Sir?"

The captain smiled. It was Sam, just as he had expected. "Sam, what can I do for you?"

"You know..." Sam said. "I came for the mail. Anything for my uncle?"

The captain had already begun looking through the pile of mail that he kept with him. The ocean liner was the only means that brought the mail to Mackinac Island, and it was a duty he was careful to carry out properly.

"Ah ha!" the captain held up a couple letters. "For the lighthouse keeper." He handed them to Sam, who took them carefully.

"Thank you, sir!"

Then Sam was off again. This time, he moved in the same direction as the passengers, dodging through them. Strangely, he ran into Grace again, but this time she dropped her suitcase, and the contents spilled out all over the ground.

"Sorry..." Sam said, stooping to help her gather up her stuff.

A letter started to flutter away. He caught it and held it out to Grace, a blush rising on his cheeks.

Grace took the letter and awkwardly stuffed it into her pocket. She was blushing, too. Now everything was contained in the suitcase again.

Sam held out his hand to her, "I'm Sam..."

"Grace Happs," she answered, shaking his hand.

They stood there looking at each other for an awkward moment, until a voice called out Grace's name.

"Grace?" It was an elderly woman.

Grace turned at the sound.

"Grace Happs?" the woman called again.

Grace waved at the old woman, who she assumed to be her aunt. The woman had a soft expression, though she looked tired.

Grace held nothing back. She smiled big and waved again. Then she turned back to Sam, "It's my great aunt..."

But Sam was already gone – he had disappeared in the crowd.

Her aunt was next to her now, and she hugged Grace. "Welcome to Mackinac Island, my dear."

Honestly, in the environment of the island, Grace expected her aunt to lead her to a horse-drawn carriage, but instead, she led her to a worn out Chevy.

"It's not much," her aunt explained, "but it takes me where I want to go."

Grace climbed into the passenger seat, and they drove away from the pier.

...

Sam had taken off as soon as Grace's aunt had appeared. He had letters to deliver, and he liked to do it as quickly as he could. His cheeks still glowed from the embarrassing encounter with Grace. Sam ran back up the beach towards the lighthouse. This time he was more wary of the tides so as to be sure to keep the letters safe.

When he arrived at the house, Sam ran into the kitchen where his uncle was sitting down to breakfast. The scent of coffee was strong in the air. Toast and eggs and fish were served on the table. Sam got right into his chair and started piling food onto his plate.

"The ocean liner came this morning. These were for you," Sam said, with food already in his mouth. He stopped eating for a second as he withdrew the letters from his pocket.

His uncle took the letters, which were slightly rumpled but dry. He smoothed them out without a comment, smiling a little. The letters were ordinary enough, just bills and more bills actually. Living in the lighthouse wasn't cheap, but Sam's uncle was good at keeping food on the table and the lighthouse from falling into mortgage.

Sam's uncle was responsible, which was a requirement for being the lighthouse keeper. He had learned the skills from his father, and now he was dutifully doing his best to teach these skills to Sam, in hopes that he would one day become the lighthouse keeper himself. His uncle often spoke of the day when he would leave and never return. Sam hated it when he talked about this, but he always listened somberly. Truth be told, Sam's uncle wasn't really his uncle – he had adopted the boy when he was just a child, and they both had no clue as to who his true parents were.

Sam's uncle looked up him from the letters. Sam was eagerly swallowing food, without hardly chewing. His uncle knew that this meant he had plans for the morning. It was July, which meant that school was out, and Sam was free to spend the time as he pleased.

His uncle cleared his throat and asked, "What?"

The single word was enough of a question because Sam knew exactly "what" his uncle was asking about.

Sam swallowed, and then started to explain, "Well... I was going to go down to the beach and..." He paused and let the sentence trail off, implying that he didn't want to explain further.

His uncle smiled knowingly and nodded. Then he said, "Just be sure you're back by noon."

"I will..." Sam answered quickly. By now Sam was finished with his breakfast. Jumping up, he left his chair ajar and ran out the door. His uncle just shook his head as the screen door closed with a click.

...

At first, Grace was a little wary of the car. She had felt a little nervous in cars ever since the accident, and she knew that it would be a while before she'd be completely at ease in a car again. But on the roads here on the sleepy island, Grace felt a calmness that she hadn't felt since the accident. She'd forgotten how good it was to feel safe.

The long roads wound through glades of forests and open fields. There were parks with benches and gazebos. They passed several houses scattered here and there through the fields and trees. Everything felt peaceful.

Grace watched as butterflies flitted among the flowers in the meadows and as the birds flew from tree to tree. The sky remained a pure blue, completely cloud-free. It was a beautiful morning, the perfect morning to be introduced to her new home on the island.

There was little talk in the car, and Grace didn't mind. The silence left her time to focus on her surroundings, which she couldn't seem to take in completely. There was too much!

Through the trees, which had little to no underbrush, Grace could see the ocean peeking at her. She wanted to feel the waves and the sand. She'd never been to a beach like this before. In New York, the places by the ocean had been dirty and full of traffic, nothing like they were here. The water looked so blue and inviting.

Suddenly Grace's aunt shifted, seeming to break from her own inner thoughts. "I'm sorry," she said. "I'm not used to having people around." She smiled sadly before continuing, "I guess I've just been alone for... too long."

"It's all right. I understand – really I do," Grace said looking up at her aunt. Their eyes met for a second before her aunt turned to look at the road again.

Now her aunt had a real smile as she said, "You can call me Aunt Clarenne."

WHITE HOUSE ON A HILL

Silence fell again, and the car drove past a row of white fencing, with climbing morning glories strewn across them. They were lovely in the morning light.

"How much farther is it – to your house?" Grace asked.

"Oh, not far," Clarenne answered.

The Chevy drove down the road and came to a fork. After taking the turn towards the right, the road climbed. At the top of the road, a white house appeared on the hill beyond.

"This is it," Aunt Clarenne said.

The drive before the house had several trees along it. They canopied over the car, casting shadows that raced across the windshield. As they approached the house, Clarenne turned the car and brought it to a stop.

Grace climbed out and looked the house over. By now, the day had warmed to more of a regular July weather, but the large oak tree beside the house still cast the front of the house in shadow. From the outside, at least, it was a beautiful house – sort of old-fashioned looking. There were two stories, and it looked as if there was an attic with some sort of balcony above that. The whole house was white, fading a little, but it still looked like it was in decent shape.

Clarenne led the way up the porch stairs, into the house.

Upon entering, the first room was a front room. There were mirrors on the wall, a large painting of the bay on another wall, and a chandelier hung from the ceiling. A large, ornate rug adorned the varnished, wooden floor. There were a few chairs and couches and a mini-grand piano stood at one end. Almost everything was white in the room. White drapes hung over the window beside the piano, and the sunlight drifting in through the window seemed to make the white drapes glow in their aura of light.

Clarenne waited patiently as Grace took in the room. Finally she asked, "What do you think of it?"

"It's beautiful..." Grace said.

"I don't have a T.V. or a computer. Those things are too modern for the likes of me. But we do have running water and electricity," Clarenne stated. To further prove her point, she flipped on the light switch and lit up the chandelier, which cast the room in warm yellow light.

Clarenne then led the way from room to room. The halls were adorned with paintings and other things. In the living room, an anchor hung on the wall. "That belonged to my father's boat – the Portlyn," she explained. "When the ship went out of use, he brought the anchor here to remember the boat by."

Shells were strewn across the mantle-piece, another rug lay in front of the fireplace, and a rocking chair sat at one side. The room had bookshelves and

more windows with more drapes. A round h.
hung above the mantle, etched with figures of she.
and starfish in its ornate frame.

From there, Clarenne led Grace upstairs. There
was another hall that branched off into bedrooms.
Each room was wallpapered in light pastel colors –
pinks and blues, and all of the furniture was white.

Grace silently nicknamed the house "the white
house on a hill." It seemed like a fitting name.

"Any of these rooms can be yours. Right now, I'm
the only one who has been living in this house,"
Clarenne explained.

Grace thought of their conversation in the car. She
began to understand what her aunt had meant when
she said she was used to being alone. But she said
nothing and began looking from room to room. Each
room was truly lovely, but Grace couldn't choose one
she liked above the rest.

At last she shrugged and said, "I don't know."

"There is the attic room as well, if you want to
see it," Clarenne mentioned the room as if it hadn't
crossed her mind before.

Grace nodded. The attic room sounded interesting, almost mysterious. The thought of something
mysterious reminded her of the feeling that she had
felt when she had first seen the lighthouse. Secrets
seemed to be enfolding her. Perhaps this room in the
attic would prove to have something to do with the
mystery she would solve? It seemed a little crazy to
believe in a fictional mystery, but to Grace, in this
new world on Mackinac Island, everything and anything seemed possible.

Clarenne led Grace to the end of the hall into a closet. The door creaked loudly as it opened, as if from disuse. The closet was a small room, with a ladder that led to the attic above. Clarenne climbed first, and Grace followed.

The room, being in the attic, had walls that sloped up into the point that made up the roof of the house. Wood beams that bordered the chimney below continued up from the living room. A bed sat in the middle of the room. Both the head and the foot of the bed were made of shiny metal bars, with several banisters holding it up. Each of the bars in the banisters was topped off with a globe.

A soft rug lay beside the bed on the floor, and a low bookshelf stood at one side. The room was wallpapered with a flowery pattern of dark reds and gold. There was a chest of drawers on the wall at the end of the bed, while a dresser with an urn of water and a basket of seashells stood beside the window. But it was the window that caught Grace's attention. The window opened with full-sized doors that led out to the balcony. The view was incredible!

A flowery, one-bulb lamp hung on the wall above the bed, and another one hung above the dresser. The room was beautiful. It was the best room in the house, Grace decided.

"The walls do slant quite abruptly," Clarenne remarked, breaking into Grace's thoughts.

"I don't mind the slant. I want this to be my room..." Grace said, turning to look at her aunt.

Clarenne smiled. "You can have it if you really want it. I never was one to like this room..." Her voice trailed off, and she got a distant look as she muttered to herself, "My sister on the other hand..." Then she seemed to remember that Grace was watching her, and she just stopped in the middle of the sentence.

After a moment, with nothing being said, Grace said, "I will get my suitcase and bring it up here."

"Why yes, of course," Clarenne replied, breaking free of her reverie.

Grace climbed back down the ladder and the stairs and retrieved her suitcase from where she had forgotten it in the front room. Weaving her way back through the house was a little hard, as she wasn't quite used to it all yet. She got turned around a bit, but the house wasn't terribly large, so she didn't have too hard of a time. She was silently grateful that Clarenne didn't own a manor.

Grace lugged the suitcase up the stairs and up the ladder into her room. When she got there, Clarenne was already gone. Grace had to admit that she was grateful to have some time alone. It seemed as if there was already so much to take in, and she needed some time to let it all sit.

Really, it all seemed like a dream to Grace. She feared that at any moment, she would wake up back on the ocean liner. Everything was too perfect. Her new life seemed too peaceful, and when things are better than it seems like they should be, it's easy for one to feel as if she will be waking up soon.

But Mackinac Island really was a peaceful island, and it really was as perfect as it appeared. Its solitude from the rest of the world made it a perfect place for fishermen, writers, and painters alike. A few tourists would visit the island, but rarely, so it was claimed mostly by itself and its few residents.

Grace opened her suitcase on the bed and began rummaging through things. Everything was topsy-turvy from being dumped out at the dock. Grace preferred having the more part of her clothes hung up, so she carried a handful of clothes on hangers to the closet.

It wasn't a large closet, but it was going to be big enough for her clothes. There were lines of racks to hang clothes on and a shelf for shoes. A long mirror hung on the door. Other than that, the closet was empty, except for a big picnic basket, which held a large, red and white-checkered, picnic blanket. Grace laughed a little when she saw it. Whoever left the basket in the closet must have loved picnics.

Next, Grace moved the rest of her clothes neatly into the dresser drawers and went on to putting away her other belongings.

At the bottom of her suitcase were her books. She had several of the classics – her favorite books. Books were like friends to her. Once she read a good book, she could never let it go. She carried the books to the little bookshelf and lined them neatly on the top shelf. She ran her finger across the spine of her copy of <u>Pride and Prejudice</u>. She loved the book and had read it many times. Then she stopped at her journal, which she, regretfully, rarely wrote in. Writing had never been one of her major undertakings. Maybe that was because she had never really had anything to write about, but somehow, here on Mackinac Island, she felt like writing. Already, phrases were forming in her mind, so she took the book from the shelf and placed it on the bed stand.

Grace pulled out the jewelry box that her father had given her on her birthday. It played one of her favorite songs – "Clair de Lune." Her mother had written special words to the song, and she had sung it as a lullaby when Grace was young. With a tender smile, Grace moved the box to the dresser beside the basket of seashells.

She couldn't help but open the box for a moment. She fiddled with the earrings and necklaces inside. Then she wound the key and let the music box play its lullaby. It was a simple, ordinary sort of thing to do, but Grace hadn't anticipated what this would do to her emotionally, and she didn't expect to feel as strongly as she did.

She had never been one to cry, and when her parents had died, she had born it well, crying little for how much she felt inside, but now, listening to "Clair de Lune," the song sang to her heart, pulling at the part of it that had been torn by the death of her parents. Unhealed wounds are easily burned by abrasion, and the song was too much for her.

The tears formed in her eyes and swelled over. Without the power to hold them back, she just let them fall. Half of her wanted to close the music box and stop the music, and the other half wanted it to never end. She missed her parents so much! The tears began falling faster, and Grace covered her face. Standing there, she cried freely and let go of the emotion she'd been holding back.

Alone in her room, feeling more peace than she'd felt in a long time, she was finally able to cry the heavy, hard tears that hadn't come before. The tears somehow washed away the pain that had been weighing on her heart.

...And with the song,
And with the song,
She found the strength,
To carry on...

THE SHORES

It was late afternoon when Grace retreated from the white house. She went alone, feeling like she still needed some time to herself. She wanted to see the ocean – up close – and she wanted to walk along the beach, maybe even hunt for seashells.

The sun was brighter above. The July heat was so warm, she almost wished she'd taken a hat, but she wasn't about ready to go back. At first, leaving the house, Grace didn't quite know which way to go, and above all, she did not want to get lost, so she walked from the house up the street that her aunt had driven her down.

Ahead, she could see the ocean through several glades of trees, across a meadow. There wasn't a road to the ocean, but Grace figured that if she went this way, she was probably less likely to get lost.

Grace had left her shoes in the house, something she would've never dreamed of doing before she had come here, but the grass felt soft beneath her feet, and it seemed the natural thing to do. The meadow was filled with blue grass, and it tickled as she ran through it.

When she arrived at the glade, she was almost out of breath. It was merely a row of trees, but it offered some shade to her for a moment. She stood beneath the tree, catching her breath and looking around. Leaning against the trunk of the tree, she stared up at the sky. Through the leaves, the sun seemed to sparkle down upon her. Every once in a while, the gentle breeze would rush through the branches, making the leaves shiver and the light dance.

From where she stood, she could see all the way down to the beach. The grass went down towards the ocean, but as it came closer, the grass faded away and only sand remained. She could tell that the tide had turned away and that it soon would be returning.

Grace took off again, running down the hill towards the ocean. She couldn't wait to feel the coolness of the water on her feet. She could hear the gulls singing now. Far out on the horizon, there were a few fishing boats, lazily drifting by.

Soon she crossed over from the grass to the sand. The sand was warm, and it pushed its way between her toes. She smiled, turning around and looking back at the footprints she had left in the sand. It felt to her, as if she had already left her mark upon the island, and it felt good.

The tide was already rolling in, so Grace stopped and rolled her pants up above her shins. Then she took off, running towards the tide. When her feet hit the first of the waves, she didn't slow down. Instead, she increased her speed – running faster and faster into the waves. As the water rose higher above her ankles, she finally slowed and just stood there, enjoying the feeling as the waves rushed past her.

It was an invigorating feeling. She spread her arms out as if to hug it all. With the water moving beneath her, it almost seemed as if she was moving forward. The wind swirled her long, dark hair behind her. Closing her eyes for a moment, she breathed it all in. She felt the way she imagined a bird must feel – free and content upon the wind.

Then the tide turned and began rushing away. She laughed as it sucked the sand from under her feet. It felt almost as if she was sinking into the sand a little.

Still smiling, she turned around. Perhaps she could hunt for seashells.

She looked up and did a double take. There was a boy sitting in the grass behind her. It only took a second for her to recognize him. It was Sam – the boy from the pier. Immediately she was embarrassed. Obviously he had seen her with her arms spread out, pretending to fly. She blushed and her hand went to her chin in embarrassment. She stared at the ground and turned clumsily, to walk away.

Sam jumped up and rushed towards her. "Where are you going?"

Grace shrugged, trying to be polite amid her embarrassment. She could feel the blush in her face and kept her eyes on the ground.

"What were you doing?" Sam said walking toward her.

Still Grace didn't say anything. How could she explain her foolishness to this boy?

Sam stopped walking and just stood there for a moment with his arms folded. Suddenly, he too, felt awkward in the moment. Usually, Sam didn't like to talk to strangers, but this girl had been kind when he had dumped out her suitcase at the dock. Though he wasn't about to admit it even to himself, he kind of liked her and really wanted to get to know her better. So far, Grace hadn't walked away, and that raised his hopes of becoming friends.

He tried again, "I haven't seen you around here before... are you new?" Immediately after he had said this, Sam began thinking what a stupid question it had been. Obviously she was new – she had come on the ocean liner, and besides that, he had never seen her before, and he knew everyone on the island. Not that he had exactly talked to everyone or that he had a lot of friends.

Sam liked to observe. Only - from a safe distance. But most especially, Sam liked to observe people.

He knew who everyone was and where they spent their time. He knew when the doctor would fetch the morning newspaper, and when the old lady would take out the trash.

But Grace didn't think the question was that stupid. She thought it was kind of this boy to notice she was new. She wanted to have a friend, so she put away her embarrassment and tried to be nice. She looked up at him for a moment, and then looked away as she spoke, "Yes, I'm new. I... just moved... here." The words came out slowly and unsteadily. She glanced back up at him for a second, and a blush spread across her face again as she looked away.

Then she blurted out, "My parents died in a car accident."

Sam hadn't expected any of this. First, he hadn't expected that she would answer him, and second, he hadn't expected her parents to be gone. He had expected her to be just another tourist –one of the people who only stayed for the summer.

He surprised himself by saying, "I'm an orphan, too... My parents died when I was really little, and I was adopted by the lighthouse keeper. He's not really related to me, but I call him my uncle."

Grace, too, was surprised to learn this, and her surprise helped her forget the shyness for a moment. However, the part that surprised her the most was that Sam lived with the lighthouse keeper. He lived in the lighthouse, her lighthouse... or at least the one that she had seen from the ocean liner, and the one that she felt a connection with.

"Really?" she asked, looking up at him, trying not to let her surprise show on her face.

Sam nodded.

"I want to see the lighthouse... sometime," Grace said.

"I'll show it to you – whenever you'd like," Sam answered quickly, his face beaming. A big, friendly smile spread across his face.

"What were you doing here?" Grace changed the subject.

"Actually, I came to look for... um, well... shells," Sam said sheepishly.

"I've always wanted to hunt for shells," Grace said enthusiastically.

"It isn't very easy to find them," Sam explained.

"I bet you know all the tricks. Will you help me?" Grace asked.

"Of course," Sam said, more than willing.

...

In the next hour, Grace and Sam each collected a bag full of shiny seashells. Sam had found one that was bigger than his hand, a real treasure. They had examined it together enthusiastically for a full five minutes. Then Sam said, "Hold it up to your ear."

Grace laughed, "Why?"

"You can hear the ocean," Sam told her.

Grace put the shell to her ear and listened. It was dim, but she could hear the whooshing sounds of the ocean. She laughed again. "That's cool," she said.

"No matter where you go, it will always sing the ocean to you," Sam told her.

"Really?" Grace questioned.

"Honest," Sam said, looking at her steadily.

They just stayed there for a moment – staring at each other. Grace was the first one to realize the awkwardness of what was happening, and she looked away. She couldn't understand this strange connection she felt with this boy she barely knew.

Neither of them noticed the tide until it was upon them, and neither of them had time to stand up before it was too late. The water came rushing in and when they stood, they had been doused from the waist down. They both laughed.

"I'm drenched!" Grace squealed, in delight.

Sam laughed again.

"And it's all your fault!" Grace said, turning and giving Sam a shove. She hadn't meant to shove so hard, but being caught up in the moment, she did, and it knocked Sam backwards. He fell all the way onto his back, dunking completely under the water.

He stood up, gasping and shaking his wet bangs out of his eyes.

Grace was laughing so hard she could barely breathe.

Sam just sat there looking at her, pretending to be angry. Grace still hadn't claimed her composure. Then Sam grabbed her arm. She squealed, trying to pull away.

"Don't!" she laughed.

But it was too late. Sam pulled her down into the water.

Grace screamed as she fell, but the water hadn't dampened her spirits. When she came up, she was still laughing. Then they both sat there, just laughing, until the tide rushed away again.

"That was so bad!" Grace said, calming down at last.

"What? Getting wet?" Sam asked incredulously.

"Yes! What is my aunt going to say?" Grace laughed again.

"I don't know," Sam said.

"I don't know either," Grace admitted. "As far as I know, she's a nice person. I mean, nicer than I ever expected her to be."

They climbed to their feet.

"That's always a good thing – right?" Sam suggested.

"Right," Grace agreed. "I hope she isn't mad."

"So... now what?" Sam said, changing the subject.

"I still really want to see the lighthouse – up close, I mean," Grace said wistfully.

THE LIGHTHOUSE

It wasn't a very long walk from the beach to the lighthouse, and when they arrived, to Sam's pleasure, his uncle wasn't there.

"Where is your uncle?" Grace wondered.

"He's probably mending nets, or buying food or matches... or something like that," Sam said.

"Oh," Grace answered.

"Come on. I'll show you everything!" Sam said, taking her hand and leading her inside.

When the front door to the lighthouse opened, Grace felt a shiver – half of fear and half of excitement. The whole place was dark, but Sam dashed ahead and began turning on lights, to make the place more "presentable."

"Really... it's a cozy place," Sam informed.

"It looks like a relic, or a museum, or something..." Grace thought aloud.

Sam shrugged. He figured it was a compliment.

The first room she stood in was a coatroom. There were yellow, rubber jackets, complete with hoods and boots, hanging on the wall.

"We use those a lot – when it's really stormy," Sam told her.

"Don't you have to keep the light in the lighthouse on? Like all of the time?" Grace asked.

"Yes," Sam said, "especially when it's really stormy. The lighthouse shows the ships where the port is, so they won't hit into the rocks and break holes in the boats. If they get too close to the rocks in a storm," here Sam made a whooshing sound effect to illustrate his point, "they're swept up against the rocks, and those currents are so strong they could dash a whole boat to pieces."

Grace didn't say anything as she tried to take in the importance of the lighthouse.

Next, Sam led her on into the kitchen. It looked ordinary enough. A stove and an oven sat at one end. Cupboards lined the walls, and a large, round window sat encased between the cupboards, with a sink beneath it. In the middle of the room sat a tall wooden table with four stools around it.

It wasn't too dirty of a place, Grace had to admit, considering that Sam and his uncle were the only people who lived there. There were a couple of dishes piled in the sink, and several cobwebs under the cupboards, but overall, it was still tidy.

The next room they walked into was lined with books. "This is the library," Sam explained as he switched on the light.

In the middle of the room was some sort of old-fashioned lantern-looking thing. It cast the room in an orange hue, making everything look more ancient than it really was. A huge map hung on one of the walls – the map showed all of Mackinac Island – including all the ports and bays, as well as the roads and houses. It was somewhat out of date, Grace thought, because the map showed a lot fewer buildings at the port than she had seen when she arrived.

On the tops of the bookshelves there was a collection of many different things. There was a ship in a bottle. Grace puzzled over it a moment and then gave up trying to figure out how the boat got in the bottle. There were other, larger models of ships, huge seashells, and some other odd pieces including an old tobacco pipe, silverware, bottles... etc.

"I found most of those," Sam said, pointing proudly at the collection of oddities. "I found them in the ocean when I went scuba-diving."

With that knowledge, the pieces suddenly had new significance to Grace, as she realized that these things had all come from the bottom of the ocean.

"One of these days I'm going to find a real treasure," Sam went on. "There are so many ships that have sunk at the port. I mean, one of them has to have something really important, something that should have never been lost."

"I guess," Grace shrugged. Though it did, undoubtedly, sound exciting to find something that someone had lost on the bottom of the ocean.

Sam took her on to the sitting room. The fireplace was huge, Grace thought.

"In winter it's the only way we keep the place warm enough," Sam said. "We don't have regular heating or air-conditioning."

Grace had already noticed the no air-conditioning part. The July heat had made the whole place just a little too warm. Sam went to the window and jerked it open.

"It's a nice day outside," he said.

As Sam went around from window to window, Grace went to the mantle-piece. There was an odd-shaped jewelry box sitting there. It seemed to be made completely out of seashells. Long and skinny seashells made up the legs that held it up. A pile of seashells made the lid, and other seashells around the sides formed a sort of bowl.

Grace tried to open the box to look inside, but it was locked.

"Yeah," Sam said, seeing her interest in the box. "That thing has been there for forever. Too bad it's locked, though. I've always wanted to see what's in it. One of these days I'm gonna pick the lock or something."

"Or you could just ask your uncle for the key," Grace suggested.

Sam shrugged.

There were a couple of soft-chairs by the fireplace. A deep sea-green rug sat on the floor between them. A globe of the world stood on its stand beside a widow that now was letting in a cool, summer breeze.

At the far end of the room, there were more bookshelves. Obviously, Sam's uncle was either a reader or a book collector.

Beside the bookshelves, there was another, round window, and beside the window, stood a telescope turned towards the window.

"Is that a real telescope?" Grace asked, rushing towards it.

"Of course," Sam said. He stood beside the telescope as Grace looked through it. The window faced the vast expanse of ocean. Grace set the telescope on one of the fishing boats that was sailing out on the tide.

She laughed as she looked. "I can see the people on the boats. It's an incredible view; I can even tell what they're doing!" She looked through the telescope for a while longer, looking from boat to boat, even trying to catch a glimpse of a flying seagull through the sight.

"Come on," Sam said at last. "I haven't even shown you the best part..."

With that, Grace left the telescope, and Sam led her down to the end of the hall. There was a door. Inside was a small, round room with wooden stairs spiraling up around a metal pole.

Grace looked up. The stairs seemed to go on forever.

"Wow," she breathed. "How many steps are there?"

"Two-hundred," Sam said proudly.

"That's a long way!" Grace said.

They began climbing the stairs, one after another. Grace laughed when she stepped on the creaky step, and the sound rang out, startling her.

But sooner than she had expected, they reached the top. There was another door, which they opened. Then they stepped out of the stairwell onto a balcony.

"This view is awesome," Sam said.

"Breathtaking!" Grace added.

Looking out, the whole island was spread out before them. The lighthouse had been built up on a hill, which hill had been chosen because it was the highest point in Mackinac Island. With the height of the lighthouse added onto the height of the hill, the view truly was amazing.

From where she stood, Grace could see far out onto the ocean. The ships looked like mere specks from up here. She could see the pier and the little road that her aunt had driven down. The balcony spiraled around the lighthouse, and when Grace went to the other side of the tower, she could even see the white house.

But more amazing than that was how far the view went from there. From the lighthouse, she could see all the way across the island, to the shore on the opposite side. She could see the houses, getting smaller and smaller as they got further and further away. She could see the cars driving on the little roads. She could even see specks of children playing in the yards. She could see it all.

"Come on," Sam said at last, breaking in to her excitement. "This is just the Main Gallery. Just wait until you see the Watch."

There was another climb of stairs that led from the Main Gallery to the Watch. There was a glass door, rounded like the top of the lighthouse. Being inside the Watch made Grace think of being in a house of glass. The whole room had windows that went down to the floor. She guessed this was so that the ships could see the light better.

In the center of the room was the bulb that cast the light. "We turn it on when it starts to get dark, and then off as soon as it gets light enough," Sam explained.

Grace nodded.

"There's a lot of other stuff that we have to do, too. Like, we have to keep these windows clean, so that the light gets out, and we have to change the bulb every now and then..." Sam continued.

Grace was only half listening now because she was so entranced by the view. It really was an amazing sight! Grace noticed that the sun was beginning to fall lower in the sky.

It was then that she thought of the time. "Oh my goodness! It must be getting late. I hope my aunt isn't worried," she exclaimed. Then she laughed at herself. "It's not like me to get lost on an adventure like this, especially the first day I arrive."

Sam smiled. "You know, if you wanted to, you and your aunt could come over for dinner," he offered.

"That's a great idea," Grace said. "I'll ask."

Then Grace took off down the stairs. Sam watched from the Main Gallery and waved at her before she took off across the beach. He waited there until she was completely out of sight.

Once she was gone, Sam just sat there, watching the sunset. He knew that soon his uncle would arrive from wherever he was, and he would have to tell him about the invitation to dinner that he'd given to Grace. Sam wasn't usually one to just invite people over, but Grace was his friend, or maybe, almost more than a friend.

...

When Sam's uncle arrived at last, it was already getting late. By now, gloaming was apparent.

"Uh, I invited some guests for dinner..." Sam said uncomfortably, looking up from the table where he had set four places.

His uncle looked uninterested.

"I don't know when they'll get here, but..." Sam hurried on before his uncle cut in.

"Mind my asking who?" his uncle asked.

"Grace Happs... and her aunt," Sam said, adding her *aunt* as an afterthought.

Sam's uncle was turned away, but even so Sam noticed how his uncle stiffened when "Happs" was mentioned.

He spun around. "Did I hear you correctly? You invited Miss Happs?" he asked.

Sam nodded. "And her niece, Grace... well actually, I invited her niece... so, if her aunt says she can... I'm guessing she'll think it's all right. Grace says her aunt is nice," Sam rambled on.

Sam's uncle laughed and turned away again. "Don't expect them. Either of them."

"Why not?" Sam questioned.

"I know Miss Happs, and she prefers not to talk to me..." his uncle explained. Here he looked out the kitchen window at the ocean. He watched the drifting tides for a moment. Then he added, "She hasn't spoken to me for over sixty years."

Sam didn't understand, but clearly his uncle didn't want to explain further, so Sam didn't bother to ask, though his thoughts were racing. Sam liked to know things. He didn't like being left out in the cold. He could tell that there were unanswered questions here, and somehow, he knew he would find the answer, even if that meant he had to look for them somewhere other than his uncle. Sam had known his uncle for nearly all his life, but now he was beginning to wonder if he truly knew him.

For the first time, Sam became aware that there was something cold in his uncle's heart. There was a distance in him, and with that, was probably the reason for him keeping to himself all of these years.

His uncle didn't really have any friends, other than Captain Grey. Sam was the only one he really ever talked to, and though it sounded a little dangerous, he felt as if meeting Grace was a good thing, a really good thing. Good not just for him, but good for his uncle as well.

Unresolved problems are like forgotten nails in a piece of wood. The tide and sand may bury them in time, but they are never really gone, not until they have been found and removed. Nails aren't the best of things to run into unexpectedly, especially nails that have been rusting – for sixty years.

FORBIDDEN

Grace had a harder time finding her way home than she had hoped. The glade she had entered was farther to the south, which was an area of the island she had not seen much of. When she had passed through the glade and crossed the meadow, she found herself facing a road. Either way she looked, the road went on farther than she could see, and there were no guiding landmarks to aid her.

Not knowing what to do, Grace stood there a moment, debating her options. She honestly didn't know if she had strayed too far one way or the other, and she didn't have a clue as to which direction she needed to go, now. Finally, she chose to go along the road heading in the direction away from the lighthouse.

After a long time, the road divided into two. She guessed which road to take – hoping again that it was the right one.

...

By seven in the evening, Grace's aunt was thoroughly worried. Grace had been gone all afternoon, and it was getting late fast. She stared out the window, getting more antsy as she waited. Clarenne

Happs wasn't one for keeping calm during worried moments. Instead, she was one to think up horrible mishaps that might have happened. She was quick-witted, and that often made her quick to worry as her mind created a fury of imaginary problems.

By this time, Clarenne had decided that Grace had either been kidnapped or had drowned in the ocean, both things to which Miss Happs felt completely responsible. She should have kept a closer eye on the child – she was only fifteen.

Clarenne finally made up her mind to search for the girl, so she climbed into her car and started out down the road. She was heading straight for the coast guard's home, hoping that somehow the child would just be unconscious, and that there would still be time to rescue her.

...

It was getting dark fast. The trees had become shadows among the grays of the landscape, which had once been bright. Grace had always been afraid of the dark, and now she was beginning to worry that she would have to spend the whole night in the dark alone.

Above, a sliver of a moon was in the sky. The stars were bright, but this time, Grace felt no peace in their light. Her heart was pounding away like a rhythmic prayer, hoping that somehow she would find her way home. But that hope was vanishing with every step, for she was sure that she should have seen something familiar by now, and nothing seemed even remotely familiar.

From the lighthouse, everything had seemed so small and simple, but from here, on this road bordered by trees, everything seemed huge and overwhelming. Every now and again, the rustling of a tree branch would startle Grace. She hugged her shoulders, trying to pull together as much comfort as she possibly could.

And then there were lights – bright lights coming from directly behind her.

They were car lights.

...

Miss Happs saw the figure in the middle of the road, and, because she hadn't been expecting it, her first impression of it startled her. But on a second glance, when she realized it was Grace, she breathed a sigh of relief. "Grace Happs! What are you doing?" she demanded.

"I was trying to find my way home... and I sort of got turned around," Grace answered in confusion and relief.

"Well how do you expect to find your way in the dark? You were heading for the more populated part of the island – in directly the opposite direction of the house," her aunt's voice was stern.

Grace was silent as she climbed into the car.

Her aunt was still a flutter – half from her scare of losing Grace and being responsible and half for agreeing to adopt Grace in the first place. She had assumed that the girl would be little trouble. "You must never, ever do this again!" she stated.

Grace couldn't understand the feelings coming from her aunt. It was just an accident that she had lost her way. She hadn't meant to.

"I've already been responsible for..." Clarenne stopped cold, in too much pain to continue.

Grace had found a wound. She could see that it was like the wound in her own heart from the loss of her family. This was a deep wound in her aunt, and she dared not disturb it any further. She wanted to help her aunt calm down. "I just went down to the beach to collect sea shells."

Her aunt didn't say anything.

"It was beautiful! And I met this boy – he helped me find the shells, and then he took me to see the light-house... he lives with the lighthouse keeper..." Grace rambled on.

"You what?" Clarenne's rage was apparent as she stepped on the brakes.

"I went to the lighthouse... he invited us for dinner," Grace tried to make her understand.

"Dinner with the lighthouse keeper? Have you gone mad?" her aunt stared at her in utter shock.

Grace hadn't had any idea this sort of reaction would be possible from the kind old woman that she had first seen this morning, but obviously there was a completely different side to her when it came to the lighthouse and the keeper.

Miss Happs started driving again. "After what he... I could never!" She was panting and fighting down emotion, like one who had just seen a ghost or had a nightmare.

"I don't understand…" Grace said, and she immediately regretted it.

"I forbid you, Grace Happs, from speaking to Mr. Warner, and I forbid you from speaking to that boy!"

"But he's my only…" Grace tried, but her aunt cut in.

"I don't care. I forbid you! And if you plan to live here with me, you will do as I say!"

Here they came to the drive in front of the house. As if to punctuate her statement, Miss Happs turned the car in a sharp angle and slammed on the brakes, making them both fall forward.

Clarenne bolted from the car.

"You can't really mean to imprison me like this…" Grace tried again, running after her.

"It's only for your good, Grace. All I want is to protect you! All I want is for you to be safe!" Then her voice cracked, and she burst into a fit of tears. She ran sobbing into the house and disappeared.

Grace had been hungry until she had seen her aunt's rage. Now she felt broken. Grace ran the opposite direction of her aunt, running until she was safe in the confinement of her room.

The moon sliver was directly outside her window. Grace could see a blur of it through the tears she that was no longer holding back. Here, where no one else could see, she let them loose.

Crying a flood of tears into her pillow, Grace regretted everything. She wished she hadn't been so naïve to go out to the beach alone without telling her aunt. She wished she hadn't met Sam – he wouldn't understand why she hadn't come for dinner or why she wouldn't talk to him again. She knew she would never be able to explain.

Then she cried over the car accident, wondering why her parents couldn't have lived as she had... Grace rolled off the bed and dug through her bag for the picture of her parents. It was the last picture they had taken – the three of them together. With her finger, she traced the outline of her dad's smile. Then she cried again, burying the picture away in her drawer.

She realized, now, that she would only be able to go on if she buried the past. She had to let the past sink, broken as a ship in the waves, until it disappeared beneath all care.

...

At that very same moment, on the very same island, Sam was alone in his room. He was puzzling over the same problem, only he knew his half of the story. He didn't know why Grace hadn't come, but he believed his uncle. It probably had something to do with her aunt.

Thinking about Grace, her aunt, and the strange problem was depressing to Sam, so he decided to think of something else. Besides, Sam had better things to think about than adults and their strange ways of thinking.

He had something mysterious and exciting that he liked to puzzle over, and that was the Legend of Mackinac Island. All of Sam's life, he'd wanted to find a treasure – his very own treasure. He believed he could do it. In all of his many excursions, he had found many little treasures, but usually they were regular things that people had just lost, not "real" treasure.

Sam went to his drawer. This drawer held his treasures, and someday, he dreamed it would hold his real treasure... but then again, maybe he would have to get a safe to put that in. The treasure drawer was a little drawer that was part of a bookshelf. The drawers were built beneath the shelf and above an open dresser area. The drawer was locked – for safekeeping, and it was the safest place Sam had, though he felt it wasn't always as safe as it should be.

Sam reached up, feeling behind the decorated piece of wood that ran above the books. He had cleared out an area in the wood, and in the crevice, his key was hidden. Sam felt this was a clever spot to hide the key. He liked and marveled over clever hiding places.

After fitting the key into the lock and turning it until it clicked, Sam set the key on the dresser and opened the drawer.

He withdrew the most prized of his findings. It was a pocket watch with initials etched into the cover. "C.P." Sam was sure it had belonged to the captain of a great ship. He had found it on one of his many scuba-diving adventures. He had the ocean floor plotted out in his book – a green composition book that he carried with him frequently. It held all of his plans, his charts, and maps. He liked to think of it as being an archaeologist's notebook.

He knew that archaeologists always sketch their findings and record the locations of their findings, so that they can piece things together. Sometimes these little clues are like a trail, which leads from little clue, to little clue... and eventually to a big clue and then... a big find.

Sam had discovered a whole sunken fishing boat this way, but it was his secret. His big secret, and he didn't want anyone to steal it from him. He had thought that he could trust Grace with his secret, but now he didn't know, with her aunt and all.

Really, nothing was harder for Sam than keeping all of his secrets and finds to himself. He desperately wanted someone that he could share them with, but Sam didn't have any other friends. There were kids at school who he kind of got along with, and there were even kids who he kind of liked... But frequently, he got into fights. Being an orphan is a hard thing, and living with the lighthouse keeper made him an "odd boy." Sam's uncle hardly talked to people, and people hardly talked to him.

Sam guessed his uncle just wasn't the talking type, and there wasn't anything he could do about it, so it made no sense that the kids at school should bug him about it, but they did. Sam wished that the kids thought it was cool for him to live in the lighthouse, like Grace did, but they didn't. They thought it was weird. Sam had learned to ignore them. He didn't mind them much, and he also didn't share his secrets much.

Still holding the pocket watch cradled in his hand, he ran a finger over the initials. He wished he knew whom the watch had belonged to. One day, he thought he might be able to gather enough clues to piece things together and figure everything out.

Sam pressed the button at the front of the watch, and the lid flipped open. The watch-hands were frozen in the nine forty-five position. Sam had thought many times that this time was a clue. This was probably the exact time when the watch had fallen into the water because the water would have quickly seeped into the seams in the watch and clogged the gears, making it stop immediately, but Sam didn't know if the time happened to be in the morning or in the evening. As he had so many times before, he fathomed he would have to gather more clues to understand the story, a lot more clues.

Sam placed the watch and its chain back into his drawer and rummaged through the other contents for a moment. He had found an ornate cigarette case, which he flipped open and closed several times, enjoying the snappy "click" sound. He had also found a silver dollar from the early nineteen hundreds. There was a case of old, rusting fishing-hooks. He had those safely in a clear-plastic box, so that he wouldn't ever get stuck by one. There were other items as well. Each one, Sam knew, held a story of its own.

When he was done looking through the drawer, he closed it and locked it. Then he returned the key to its hiding place. He was tired by now. It had been a long day, with a lot of surprises, and Sam was ready to sleep.

He lay on his bed and gazed out the window over the head of his bed. Above, he could see the sliver of moon. The moon was waxing. Sam knew this because it had been disappearing for a while.

Sam liked it best when the moon was full, but tonight its shape seemed somehow appropriate. Perhaps it was that the moon reminded him of the sliver of hope he felt inside. The hope that he could figure out what was between his uncle and Grace's aunt. But more than that, it was a sliver of hope that he had really found a friend, and he hoped this sliver of hope would wax... like the moon.

Stealing Away

When the rays of morning light first streamed into Grace's room, she awoke, not knowing where she was. First, she thought she was at the orphanage. Then, she realized where she was, and a moment after that, the events of the day before came crashing down upon her like a tidal wave.

Suddenly she was tired again - too tired to get up. She wanted to stay in bed for the whole morning, maybe longer than that. She had actually found a friend - her first real friend for a long time. Then that friend had been cruelly taken away from her by her aunt, the aunt that had seemed so nice.

With the memories rising, Grace rolled over in bed and pulled the coverlet up partially over her head. Her stomach rumbled a little. She was kind of hungry, but not hungry enough to face her aunt. It didn't take long for Grace to drift off to sleep again – a peaceful sleep, far from the cruel reality.

...

On this same morning, Sam had gotten up and eaten breakfast with his uncle. It had been a quiet meal for the more part of it, but then, neither of them had ever been very talkative, so it wasn't a strange thing.

When his uncle had finished eating, he sat there a moment. Then he said, "I suggest that you leave Miss Happs and her niece to their own business for a while. Perhaps, for a long, long while."

Then his uncle had gotten up from the table and had left the lighthouse.

Sam sat at the table, alone for a moment, thinking. His uncle had suggested, but Sam didn't agree with the suggestion, and Sam didn't like being told what to do. His uncle knew that, so he rarely did so, but this was one of those rare occasions.

As Sam thought, he came up with a plan, one that he was going to execute, even if it got him in a lot of trouble. There was a chance, a very slim chance, but still a chance that he could do some good by avoiding this "suggestion" from his uncle, and so he headed off to carry out his plan.

...

Grace was in the middle of a peaceful dream. She was with Sam, riding a boat in the middle of the ocean. They were laughing, though the dream hadn't explained why. Everything was perfect, that is, until she heard a loud bang. The sound woke her with a start.

Sitting up attentively straight on her bed, she glanced around her room. Had something fallen? What had caused the sound?

Then she heard it again. It was a loud bang, and it seemed to be coming from her window. It almost sounded like something hitting the glass. She slid out of her bed and rushed to the window. Parting the curtains, she squinted at the sunlight.

There, in the front lawn was Sam Warner.

Grace was so happy she could have screamed, but at the same time, her heart was racing like crazy. She knew she wasn't supposed to talk to Sam anymore. If she did, and her aunt found out, she didn't know what would happen, and she knew that it would just make things worse, a lot worse.

But Grace also knew that she needed Sam. She needed Sam more than her aunt knew and maybe even more than Sam knew. She needed a friend. Their afternoon together, the day before, was the first time she had really been able to be herself since the accident, and she knew that he was the key to her new life. Throwing caution aside, Grace opened the glass door that led onto the balcony and walked out.

"You're not supposed to be here," she said in a harsh whisper.

"Why not?"

"My aunt said that I can't talk to you anymore," she forced the words out, fighting the desire to ignore her aunt's wishes.

"Come on. And you're gonna listen to her?" Sam was taunting.

Grace shrugged. Obviously she wasn't obeying her aunt. She avoided answering the question. "If she catches you here, it's going to be bad for both of us," she warned.

Sam shrugged. "So? Haven't you ever taken a chance? Done something daring or a little crazy?"

Grace found herself laughing. She couldn't resist. She was trying to convince him that they weren't going to be friends anymore, when she herself was wishing for the opposite.

"Okay..." she said finally. "I'll meet you on the road. Five minutes. But get out of here before you get us in trouble."

Sam agreed with that, and in a few seconds, he was out of sight.

Grace went back into her room and pulled on her shoes. She had slept in her clothes, being so upset she had fallen asleep without changing.

Once her shoes were on, she went back onto the balcony. "Now the question is how do I get down there?" she wondered. Grace knew she couldn't just go downstairs and out the door. Her aunt was probably somewhere in the house doing something, and if she went out, her aunt would demand an explanation. There had to be another way out. Now Grace was beginning to regret choosing the attic room.

She had not only chosen the highest room in the house, but also the one with the most limited exits. She had picked the most secure of the jail cells.

Standing there for a moment, she felt more daring than she had ever felt in her life. She decided that she was going to climb down from the balcony, no matter how she had to do it. She was going to. Being that decided isn't always the best thing, but it sure is powerful.

"Where there's a will... there's a way," Grace whispered.

Then, she swung her leg over the banister of the balcony. As carefully as she could, she stood on the outside edge, clinging to the railing. "Don't look down," she told herself.

It was a long way down.

Suddenly she realized that it would have been much smarter to think things through a little more before she just climbed over the balcony, but it was too late now.

The three stories weren't exactly short stories, but there was a trellis that was barely within arm's reach. The thing was covered with morning glories and climbing clematis. If Grace was careful, she knew that she could use it like a ladder and climb down the wall.

It took holding her breath, as she reached her leg away from the balcony a moment, before she had completely made up her mind. Half on the trellis and half on the balcony, Grace debated again if this was the wisest way to exit the house.

"Maybe it would be easier to just get in trouble..." she reasoned with herself. Grace thought of Pollyanna and how she had been paralyzed when she fell, which wasn't the wisest thing to think of, but the fear of the thought somehow brought her second foot to the trellis, and after that, she let go of the balcony completely.

With a final sigh of relief, she climbed down the trellis the rest of the way. When her feet touched the ground, she could have fainted in relief, but she knew Sam was waiting. She also knew that she needed to get out of sight, so she sprinted across the lawn, not stopping until she had cleared the drive and was on the far road that led to her home.

There, she found Sam.

"Well, that wasn't so bad, was it?" he said.

"You have no idea how risky that was!" Grace answered, still breathing hard from her climb and run.

"But it was worth it, right?" Sam smiled.

Grace decided this would be a good time to explain what had happened the night before. "Hey," she began, "I'm really sorry that I didn't show up last night. It was half my fault. I got lost on my way back. My aunt had to come and find me... And when she did she was pretty mad about it, but then, when she heard that I had been to the lighthouse, she went insane! She told me I couldn't talk to you anymore." Grace laughed wryly. She had just confirmed that she was deliberately disobeying her aunt, but she wasn't ashamed at all. She had never felt better telling someone something in her life.

"Yeah, my uncle kind of knew about the situation, too. When I told him I'd invited you and Miss Happs over, he got really weird. I've never seen him that way."

"There's something weird going on between them, or at least something has happened between them, and they're both still pretty upset about it," Grace reasoned.

"But why should that matter to us? Grown-ups are weird sometimes. It's their business, but it has nothing to do with us," Sam assured her.

"But Sam, it's got everything to do with us."

Sam looked puzzled.

"I mean, they don't even want us to talk because of their grudge. It's a really bad grudge! I think we need to get to the bottom of it," Grace said.

"And what, make them talk to each other? It's been sixty years! That's a long time to not be on speaking terms," Sam argued.

"Fine. Whatever," Grace said. "But I still think it's weird, and I still think we should get to the bottom of it."

To Sam, though, it was of little interest right then. "All right, we can solve your mystery, but some other time. I got you for a reason, and it wasn't to talk about depressing stuff. I wanted to talk about better things – things more worth your while."

"Okay, I'm all ears."

Sam looked around nervously for a moment. "You might be all ears, but there might be other ears listening as well. It's not safe here."

"Okay, you're really starting to freak me out."

Sam laughed softly. "I mean it. It's a big secret – my big secret, and I haven't told anyone about it. Not a single, living soul."

"Not even your uncle?" Grace's eyes widened.

"Not even him. Nobody."

Grace took this as a compliment. He trusted her with his secret. "Okay, so where do we have to go so we can be *safe*?"

"Why don't we go back to the lighthouse? My uncle's not there, and I don't think he's coming back for a while, so the lighthouse is ours," Sam said.

"Maybe you should teach me the way to the light-house from here. I sort of needed that yesterday," Grace suggested.

...

They walked down the first road for a while. Soon the road came to a bend, and there was a weathered road that turned off of it. It clearly hadn't been driven on for a while. Grass had grown up all over it. The thing that made it the most visible was the sagging gate that crossed its way.

Sam was the first to climb the gate. He made it look almost effortless with his long legs. It was clear to Grace that he had a lot of practice with gate climb-ing. She was a little slower at it, but it was still simple enough.

Beyond the gate, there was a clearly marked path. It was a mostly wooded area, with grass that grew on the trail. They followed the path until the trees gave way. As they did, Grace realized that the lighthouse was in sight.

Sam had a shortcut, and knowing this made Grace feel almost as if the lighthouse and the white house on a hill were connected.

"So, now can you tell me about your secret?" she whispered.

"Well we're not exactly at the lighthouse yet."

"But you don't seriously think there's somebody around," Grace argue.

"You can never be too careful," Sam said cautiously, and with that, he led the way across the field.

Running alongside Sam, Grace almost felt like a bird gliding over the meadow. The morning was as beautiful as the day before had been. The sky was a brilliant blue, with a few feathered clouds above. The summer grass never smelled sweeter.

The Legend of the Silver Pearl

In little to no time, they had reached the lighthouse, and once the door was shut behind them, Sam turned to Grace. "Okay, cyou can't tell anyone about this. Okay?"

"Well, yeah," Grace said.

"So you won't?" Sam persisted.

Grace gave him a serious look. "No, I won't tell anyone unless I absolutely have to, or unless it would be the best thing to do."

"What's that supposed to mean?" Sam asked.

"I mean, I won't tell anybody, unless for some reason I need to. Like what if you got lost and they were looking for you, and I had a good idea of where you were. Then I would tell them so that you would be found," Grace explained.

"Well, that won't happen," Sam reassured her.

"All right then," Grace folded her arms impatiently.

"Okay, okay," Sam said. "There's this legend about Mackinac Island. It's a really old legend, and a lot of people don't believe it... but I do."

Grace nodded. Though she wasn't showing it outwardly, she was beginning to worry that Sam had gone mad.

"It's the Legend of the Silver Pearl," he continued.

"And what does the legend say?" Grace encouraged.

"Well, um, it's sort of just that the pearl was lost somewhere on Mackinac Island, or that someone hid it... or something happened to it."

"If you ask me, it sounds like more than just the pearl is hiding," Grace said.

"Like what?" Sam asked.

"Like the rest of the legend. I mean, if you're going to try to find something, you've got to gather clues, and it seems to me that the first thing you would want to find would be the most reliable source of the legend so that you could track down how it all started. If you don't do that, you could be off on a wild goose chase trying to find something that doesn't and never did exist."

"You have a point," Sam agreed, sitting down on one of the stools in the kitchen. "So, what do you suggest we do?"

"Well, where did you first hear about the Legend of the Silver Pearl?" Grace asked.

"I don't know," Sam shrugged. "I think it's an old fisherman's tale. Everybody on the island knows it. It's kind of like a fairy tale around here."

Grace wasn't convinced. "So what makes you so big on finding it? And how do you have any proof it's even real? It's clear that not everyone is as anxious about the sliver pearl as you are. This is the first time I've heard anything about it."

Sam hadn't expected Grace to be so to the point. Usually the first thing you had to do in order to find an answer was to ask the right question, and Grace had all of the questions, but Sam hadn't wanted to give away the source of his story, not yet at least. He had been planning to keep this part of the secret to himself.

However, now that had she asked, and now that he had included her in his search, he knew he'd better tell her – all of it.

Grace kept pressing, "So, was it a story that you heard? Or something you read somewhere? Or..."

"All right, I'll show you, but you really can't tell anybody about this. Okay?" Sam pleaded.

"You've already sworn me to secrecy," Grace reminded him.

"If you call that sworn," Sam responded.

"It's the best promise that you'll ever get from me. My dad taught me never to promise anything that I can't keep, so I never promise complete silence. I keep the right to tell, but only in completely necessary cases. You have nothing to fear – unless you stole something." Grace looked concerned. "Then I'd have to tell."

"I didn't steal anything," Sam said. "And I've never stolen anything. I'm not a robber. I'm a treasure hunter."

"Great," Grace smiled.

Sam soberly led Grace to his room, right up to the bookshelf. He didn't want Grace to see where he hid the key, so he said, "Close your eyes."

Grace obeyed, and Sam retrieved the key from its crevice. He unlocked the drawer and took out the pocket watch. "Hold out your hand," he said.

Grace did as she was told, and Sam dropped the pocket watch into her hand. Immediately she opened her eyes. "Where did you get this?" she breathed.

"I found it. I have the precise x-y coordinates on my graphed out map of the ocean, but to make it simple, I found it on the bottom of the ocean."

"Did you have to go very deep? I mean, this is a rare thing to find, isn't it?" Grace questioned.

"Well, actually, it was somewhat close to the shore, not too far from the lighthouse."

"Amazing," Grace breathed again.

Then, she instinctively pressed the button on the watch, and the lid popped open. "It's just as ornamental inside of here. It's so fancy. I think it's a shame for whoever lost it," she spoke wistfully.

Sam wondered if she would notice the writing. It was small text on the lid, and it had taken Sam weeks to discover it. Actually, it wasn't until he was drawing sketches of the watch for his notebook that he had discovered it.

"What is this writing on the lid?" she asked.

Sam was impressed.

Grace continued, "There's some tiny writing on the lid? What does it say?"

"I was wondering when you'd notice it," Sam said, not mentioning, of course, how long it had taken him to find it.

"It's tiny, and so easy to miss," Grace justified.

"But yet so critical."

"Okay, you're talking weird now, Sam. What's up?"

Sam hadn't noticed his personality change, but whenever he was around his findings, or on the search for more lost items, his imagination made him feel almost scholarly – years older than he truly was, and his mouth began trying to come up with fancy words to use.

"Did you read it?" Sam changed the subject.

Grace turned the pocket watch towards the window until the words glinted in the light and read:

> "Beyond the lighthouse,
> Across the sea –
> A forgotten cove
> Awaiteth me.
> Be it dark,
> Or be it bright,
> The Silver Pearl
> Will I bring to light..."

"What's that supposed to mean?" Grace asked.

"That's what I'm not exactly sure about."

"Me neither, but this still doesn't prove the legend is a real thing. I mean, if no one has ever found it, then is it real?" Grace questioned.

"It's got to be real!" Sam said, getting ready to argue. This was one of the reasons why he hadn't told anybody about his plans and his find – because they would think he was crazy, but he wasn't. He knew he wasn't – the sliver pearl was out there waiting for him.

"So, what's your plan?" Grace asked.

"Are you in? I mean, you're really going to help me?" Sam hadn't expected this.

"If you're positive it's not just a wild goose chase, then I'm in."

"Well, I'm almost positive..." Sam started before Grace cut in.

"So, what are we going to do?" she asked.

Sam reached into his drawer and pulled out his green notebook. He had pasted in a piece of paper to act as a pocket directly inside the front cover of the book. In this pocket was where he kept his map. He unfolded it carefully and spread it out across the wooden floor.

"This is my map. I have all of my findings plotted out on it. It's as accurate as I could get it."

Grace looked it over. The map looked practical enough. The lighthouse was at one side, and the cliffs were on the other. The pier, where she had first arrived at Mackinac, was just beyond the cliffs. In between these, was the long, open beach. Sam had this area all plotted out with lines that intersected each other. It was a grid. The line that went directly through the lighthouse was his meridian line: where 0 was on the x-axis. And then the line across the beach was where 0 was for the y-axis. From there, he had lines evenly spaced, marking that each one was roughly twenty feet apart.

Grace noticed that there were colored dots all over the map, and each dot had a tiny number next to it. "What are the dots?"

"The dots are where I found something, and they're color coded by how big or important they are. Red dots are where I found my best things. Yellow is second best. Green is third best. Blue is just average stuff, and purple is basically random pieces of garbage – you know, bottles and stuff." Sam enjoyed explaining his map.

Grace observed that there were very few red dots, and there were a lot of purple dots. Obviously Sam hadn't found a lot of things that he considered really great finds.

"How about the numbers, what are they for?" Grace asked.

"In my notebook, I have all of the items cataloged." Sam flipped his composition notebook open to a page in the middle.

In the top corner of the page was a number. Across the top in nice print, he had written the name of the item, its x-y coordinates and the date and time in which he had discovered the item. Below that, he had drawn the image in as much detail as possible, and below that was an explanation on the item – how the thing was buried, or how he had come across it, or other notes that he thought were necessary.

"Very impressive," Grace admitted.

And it was. Sam felt a sense of pride in how carefully he had logged everything. For the first time in his life, he was able to show it to someone, someone he trusted his treasure-hunting secrets with, and it felt good. In fact, the secrets almost felt safer now with Grace knowing, than they had when he was the only one who knew.

"So the pocket watch is number 74, and looking at your map, I can tell that you found it somewhere around sixty feet from the shore," Grace observed.

"You got it," Sam smiled.

Grace read the text again from the notebook. It was easier to read there. She couldn't help but notice that Sam had aligned the words in the same strange way they had been aligned in the pocket watch.

"A forgotten cove... it seems that this message is hinting that there's some sort of cove, or cave or something, and the pearl is hidden inside of it. Do you know of any caves around here?" she asked.

"Caves? No."

"Have you ever looked before?" she asked.

Sam shrugged. "Not really."

"I think this is talking about a cave, and a lot of caves are formed from the waves crashing against cliff walls," Grace mused.

"We should check the cliffs then," Sam said jumping up.

UP THE TRELLIS

By late afternoon, they had been up and down the cliffs. First they observed from above, then, when the tide was away, they checked along the beaches, but it was all to no avail.

"Well, so much for that idea," Grace said.

The search had exhausted them both. They began to feel hungry again, even though they had eaten peanut butter sandwiches for lunch.

"I wonder if I should be getting home now," Grace admitted. "I don't want my aunt to even think that I have left the house."

"Good luck with that. Do you think you can find your way back by yourself?"

Grace laughed. "Yeah, I think I'm all right this time." She turned to walk back up the beach.

"Hey," Sam caught up with her. "Will you be able to come tomorrow?"

Grace thought a moment. "I don't know. I might need to do some other things, so that my aunt won't be suspicious."

"Well, what about at noon tomorrow?" Sam pressed.

Grace smiled, realizing Sam needed a friend as badly as she did.

"All right, I'll meet you at the lighthouse around noon tomorrow, but only if everything goes all right. If my aunt is suspicious of anything, then I'll come the day after tomorrow. Okay?"

"That works," Sam said.

With that, Grace turned and took off running up the beach.

Sam had quite a ways to go as well, and once he was alone, he continued walking along the beach. He loved doing this, though it wasn't very productive, he had to admit, but it made him feel good. Of course, it wasn't completely wasted time because while he walked, the wheels in his head were spinning double-time.

There was another secret that Sam was deliberating about sharing with Grace. In his discoveries the week before, Sam had found a sunken ship. It wasn't terribly far from the shore, but it was a good distance. From his brief observations, he guessed that the boat had somehow gotten out of control during a storm. It was dangerously close to the rocks along the shore, and it seemed likely for the ship to sink there.

Sam didn't know how long the ship had been rotting away or how old it was, but from the style of the boat, he guessed that it could be a century old at least, which made it even more exciting to Sam. He had been arranging to borrow a boat and some scuba-diving equipment from one of his uncle's few friends.

He thought of the tall, strong-built sailor who had softened with age. Everybody called him Captain Gray. He was the manager of the boating dock, down beyond the pier. His gray beard jutted out in disarray, and his bushy eyebrows waited above his twinkling eyes. He liked to wear the old, fishermen-styled cap and scarf. Sam didn't know for sure, but he guessed that he still went out fishing by himself every now and again.

In his mind, Sam had a plan. All of the details were worked out, and if Grace showed up tomorrow, it would work. It would work perfectly. All he had to do was hope that Captain Grey would agree. That was the one missing piece.

...

Grace found her way easily, using the shortcut that Sam had taught her. It was a simple route and easy to follow. Grace only hoped that her aunt hadn't gone up to her room to check and see whether or not she had been there. Grace never lied, though in this case she was afraid that she would have to make up a story, but she didn't want to do that.

She hoped with all of her heart that her aunt would think she was so upset that she had stayed in her room all day – that was what she hoped. She didn't want to have to explain. She didn't want to have to explain anything.

Soon she had arrived on the other side of the trail through the forest glade, meeting up with the sagging gate. She climbed over it and hurried up the last stretch of road in front of her aunt's drive.

When she reached the white fence that she recognized as "home," with the same, fading white mailbox that stood in front, she stopped for a moment, thinking it would be wise to plan ahead before she tried to execute something.

As she stood there catching her breath, she tried to think of as many excuses as she could – places she could have gone, things she could have seen. Finally, when she felt she was ready for anything, she started up the drive.

It was a beautiful walk, now that Grace was taking the time to notice it. She had figured that if her aunt saw her out the window, it would be good for her to be walking instead of running, so she was strolling casually down the path, staring up at the trees and at the sky.

A mocking bird called down to her with an unusual call. Several sparrows flew from tree to tree or hopped along the ground hunting for seeds. The sky still had those feathery clouds. They were so few and so sparse that the day couldn't be called cloudy, but they were still there.

It was another beautiful day on the island. Grace wondered if the island ever had bad weather. It seemed like the weather would change, but the two days she had spent there had all been bright, and really, they seemed to be the first bright days she had seen for quite a while. New York was unusually rainy in the weeks before she had left, and her emotions had seemed to match the weather.

By now, she reached the house, completely uncertain as to whether or not her aunt had actually seen her out the window. Grace decided that it would be the safest to return to her room the same way she had left – up the trellis.

She carefully climbed, rung by rung, until she had reached the top. Then she carefully stepped onto the balcony and swung one leg over the guardrail and then the other. She was home.

Inside her room, she sat on her bed for a moment, breathing long sighs of relief. Though she knew it wasn't over until her next encounter with her aunt, she was free for the moment. Once Grace's fears had subsided, she looked down at her pants. Her clothes were filthy. She was caked, head to toe, in sand.

Grace decided it would be best if she took a bath – to hide all evidence.

...

After a long, hot bath of relaxation and sand removal, and once the bottom of the bathtub had no trace of sand left in it, Grace went back into her room and sat on her bed again.

The clock on her dresser told her that she probably had a couple hours before dinner, so she decided to put the time to a good use. She took her diary off of the nightstand and opened it to a blank page. She wanted to write about her adventures, about what Sam had shown her, and about her aunt. She had a lot that she wanted to write about, but suddenly she was afraid that her aunt might possibly snoop in her diary.

Then Grace got an idea. She flipped to the back of the book and started writing on the back of the last page. This way, if anyone snooped, her latest entries would be at the very back – missed.

The first few words were hard for Grace to choose. She hadn't done much writing on her own, and whenever she had written in her diary before, it had always sounded mundane and robotic. This time she hoped things would be different. She hoped that she could somehow capture the moments in words and spin them into an interesting account.

And slowly, as more words filled the page, they began to flow more quickly into her mind. Sooner than she had expected, the words were cramming into her thoughts so fast, it was all she could do to keep up with them.

By the time she looked up, after the seventh page, she noticed it was getting dark outside.

It was time for her to face her aunt. Good or bad, it was time.

This time, instead of just setting her diary on the bed stand, Grace slid it underneath her pillow. This way, she figured it would keep even the snoopers away.

As she climbed down the steps that led to the lower level of the house, she could already smell food from the kitchen. She was unusually hungry, but the tension building up inside of her was quickly muting out her hunger.

She made her way down the stairs, through the hall, and into the kitchen. Her aunt was waiting for her, sitting at the table. She looked up when Grace came in.

"Hello, Darling," she said suddenly, and she flashed a smile at Grace.

Grace's mind was quick to brush off the gesture as being insincere, but it wasn't. It was a very real smile. It told Grace two things: one, her aunt wasn't mad at her anymore; and two, her aunt hadn't seen her leave the house.

"Did you rest all right? You really kept to yourself all day..." her aunt started.

"I'm fine," Grace said.

"I guess you had a lot to think about, as I did. Grace, I'm sorry about how rudely I treated you last night. I never like to get unhappy with people, especially when they make honest mistakes. I make mistakes too, you know, but I was meaning to explain to you how... you already know, and we don't need to discuss this further."

Her aunt rubbed her forehead and sighed as if she had a headache. She turned towards the window and stared out, "Sometimes I wonder why the past can't just die. It's like it tries so hard to hold onto you, like the skeleton branches in autumn that rattle in the wind without the summer leaves. Sometimes it's hard to get away... and sometimes you just can't let go."

"And sometimes," Grace said. "You just have to rip away from them." She said the word "rip" with such force that it did exactly as the word implied, except it ripped her aunt right out of her daze.

"Nicely said, Grace."

"Thanks," Grace smiled.

Grace took the seat across from her aunt and began to eat. It was a humble meal: green beans, hot rolls, and clam chowder. The chowder, Grace had to admit, was wonderful. It wasn't too fishy or too strong with potato flavor. The potatoes had been cooked to their ultimate softness, and the onions and clams blended with it all so perfectly. It was truly a masterpiece of flavor.

"The soup is great," Grace said.

"Thank you," her aunt blushed a little. "It was my mother's recipe."

...

When dinner had been cleaned up, and Grace had gone back up into her room, she felt a new relief. Everything seemed so bright again. Though her aunt still hadn't given her permission to talk to Sam, she felt like her aunt did care about her – because of her apology.

Everybody has moments, Grace knew, to be overwhelmed by feelings. But what Grace hadn't realized before was that in every one of those moments of agitation, the way the person reacts can completely change a relationship. Every action adds up to what you are.

The exchange with her aunt at dinner had nearly mended everything. All of the hard feelings that Grace had once felt towards her aunt were currently soothed, and this is what made Grace realize how tangible the balance was. Every moment counts.

DEEP SEA

Early the next morning, Sam was up with the sun. He knew exactly where he was headed and what had to happen. What he didn't know was if it would happen. Right now, as he ran across the beach, the only thought in his mind was, "Execute the plan."

He hoped that things worked out for Grace, but it was hard for him to know. He wouldn't know a thing until noon, so instead of worry and puzzling over what he would do if Grace didn't show up, he made up his mind that she would make it. If she couldn't, well, it wasn't up to him, so the best he could do was just forget about it.

Sam wasn't a worrier, especially when he couldn't do anything, but even in times when he could do things, he didn't worry. His reflexive thoughts were always fast, no panic. In emergencies this was a good thing, no panic – quick results.

...

Soon enough, by the time Sam passed the pier, the sun was casting long shadows across the island. There weren't any ocean liners this morning, and even if there had been, Sam wouldn't have cared much.

When he reached the pier, Sam slowed to a walk. It was only a short distance to the docks where Captain Grey's cabin was. It was a little house, built high up on breakers so that if the waves got out of control, his house wouldn't be washed away.

With the cabin in sight, Sam noticed the thin curl of smoke that rose from Grey's chimney, making it apparent that Grey was inside. Sam knocked on the door three times and waited.

All at once, the door burst open, and Grey was standing there. "What do you want?" his burly voice burst out of the cabin.

Someone who didn't know Grey would have been frightened off at this, but Sam knew Grey's soft side, so it didn't scare him.

"Oh, Sam – how can I help you?" Grey said quickly, his voice softening. He smiled broadly.

"I need your help with something..." Sam said.

Grey's eyes sparkled like a fellow conspirator as he let Sam in, and they both sat at the table. The little cabin was only two rooms. There was the main room, with a bed and a stove, and then there was Grey's office – a little room cluttered with papers. The whole cabin was cluttered, but it still felt cozy.

"I found a sunken ship," Sam explained.

"Another one?" Grey was interested.

"It's not far off the coast – just a couple hundred feet or so. I'm guessing it's almost a century old. It's an older boat..." Sam went on.

"And what, if I can ask, do you want to do with this boat?" Grey asked, a twinkle in his eye.

"Come on, Grey... you know..." Sam said.

Grey laughed a loud, hearty laugh. "You're right, Sam, I do know. I always know. You want me to take you out there so that you can explore. Right, eh?"

"That's it."

"You're sure one of them treasure hunters at heart. Never can settle for one piece of information, can you?" Grey teased.

"Well, I would be happy with any of my finds, except they always hint of more finds. You know, one clue leads to the next. Every answer I find, leads to a million more questions," Sam laughed again.

A giant smile spread across Grey's face again. "There's nothing better than a little adventure these days. It's one of the few things that can make you feel young again. You somehow know how to get to me, boy." Grey laughed again. "So, when will we leave? Is this another trip that stays just between us?"

Sam nodded. "Yup. My uncle doesn't need to know..."

"What's your uncle got against you treasure hunting?" Grey asked.

"I don't know. Maybe he doesn't have anything against it, but for now it seems best if I just keep it to myself. He just gets so quiet sometimes, and strange, and I don't know what I'd do if I had to stop. It'd be torture."

"Kind of like keeping a sailor on land," Grey agreed. "All right. It'll be our secret."

"We'll leave from the lighthouse at noon. Oh, and I have a friend I want to bring along," Sam mentioned as if it were of little importance.

"Now wait a minute! A friend? You! I didn't think you had any friends – at least, none that you trusted enough to take on your escapades."

Sam smiled. "I've finally found one."

...

Grace hadn't planned on sleeping as long as she had, but it felt good to be able to sleep peacefully. She hadn't cried herself to sleep the night before, and just the thought of things being all right with her aunt made Grace relieved.

She sat up and stretched. The scent of coffee was strong in the air, and for a moment she just sat there, taking everything in. She had left her window open all night, and now her whole room had a fresh scent, mingled with the scent of coffee that she had noticed earlier.

As her mind became less groggy, she remembered her promise to Sam. She had to figure out a way to get out of the house around noon so that she could meet Sam at the lighthouse. Grace remembered the picnic basket from her closet, and immediately, she started getting ideas. She almost felt like an agent undercover or something, and she needed a disguise. She chose a long dress from her closet – it seemed like it would do the trick.

Grace loathed wearing dresses. She only did it when she absolutely had to, and she felt like this was one of those moments because she *had* to in order to keep her aunt from getting suspicious. For the first time ever, she felt like she'd actually found a good use for a dress. She giggled a little at herself, thinking how ridiculous the plan seemed. This was definitely something Sam didn't have to know about.

Once Grace was ready, she looked at herself in the mirror to be sure she looked convincing enough, and then she went downstairs, taking the large, picnic basket from her closet.

Her aunt looked up from the newspaper she was reading when Grace entered, "Nice to see you this morning, Grace."

Grace smiled, setting her picnic basket down next to the table.

"Did you sleep all right?" Her aunt folded her newspaper and set it on the table. It was obvious that she wanted to have conversation.

Grace nodded.

Clarenne sipped her coffee carefully.

Grace took a bite of toast and sip of orange juice. Her aunt was silent.

"I was wondering if I could go on a picnic today. There are a lot of nice fields around here, and I want some time outside," Grace begged, trying not to sound too urgent.

Grace could see the question in her aunt's eyes, and she watched as she fought it back.

"That sounds wonderful, dear," she said, a little forced.

"I like spending time outside. It's great to hear the birds and watch the clouds, and with school out for the summer, I should have lots of time," Grace went on, keeping up the cover of her real reason to want to be outside.

Her aunt's smile grew and Grace realized that she had convinced her. It had worked – her plan had been a success.

As soon as they finished their chat, and Grace had packed a lunch in her basket, she walked slowly out the door. Of course this was a show, and as soon as she felt she was a safe distance away, she darted down the path.

Outside the fence, hiding behind a bush, Grace ripped off the dress to the t-shirt and shorts she had been wearing underneath. Her aunt hadn't suspected a thing.

Grace stuffed the dress under the food in the picnic basket, and raced down the road.

...

It was closer to eleven o'clock when she reached the lighthouse, but Sam was more than happy to see her.

"You made it!" Sam said. He had been sitting on the porch, debating what he would do if she hadn't shown up.

"Yup," Grace said. "And I brought us a picnic, too."

"Wow! How'd you convince your aunt to that?"

"It was all part of the plan," Grace beamed.

There wasn't a lot of food, as Grace had hoped not to make it seem like she was getting food for two, but they were happy to share what was there. They didn't need the blanket because they just ate on the porch steps.

"So, what's up for today? Have you found out anything else about the pearl?" Grace asked.

Sam shook his head and smiled mysteriously. "But there's something that I've wanted to do."

"What?"

Just then, Grace noticed a fishing boat approaching the lighthouse dock. "Who is that?" she asked.

"That's Captain Grey with our ride," Sam explained.

"What? We're going out on the ocean?"

"We're going scuba-diving. I found a shipwreck that I want to explore," Sam's eyes shone.

"Honest?"

Sam nodded.

Grace was so excited she could hardly contain herself. They hurried to clean up their food, Grace hurrying faster than Sam.

When Sam opened one of the sides of the basket, he noticed Grace's dress underneath the picnic blanket.

"What's this?" Sam asked, beginning to pull it out with a teasing smile.

Grace slammed the basket shut on his hand.

"Something..."

THE LOCKET

waIt wasn't long before Sam, Grace, and Grey were speeding across the water. It was exhilarating to Grace. The ocean liner hadn't been anything like this little motorboat.

Sam was busy with a map and periscope, trying to locate the sunken ship.

As the boat came closer to the cliffs, the boat slowed down. Soon Sam could see the sunken ship in his periscope.

"I found it!" he shouted.

"Let me see," Grace took the eyepiece of the periscope and gazed into it.

The ocean looked gloomy, and the sight of the boat looked haunting. She shivered as she looked. It wasn't a very big boat. She guessed that it must have been just an old fishing boat, but it looked as if it had been there forever. The bottom of the boat had rotted through in the middle, and moss covered the sides. Rubbish surrounded it, and Grace was sure Sam intended to sort through it.

"All right," Grace said, not totally thrilled at the idea of sorting through junk.

Sam was already suited up when she looked back. "Come on," Sam mumbled through his mask. Then he went to the side of the boat and rolled backwards into the water.

It took Grace a while to get suited up, and Grey had to show her how to put everything on. Then when she jumped in, it was a half fall half jump. But she was in the water, and it was amazing! With the goggles on, she could see everything so well.

Breathing underwater felt strange, though, because all of the weight of the water was on her lungs, but it was all right. Grace clumsily swam to catch up with Sam. He had immediately started looking through the rubble. They each had a bag to put the things they found in, and Sam had already found an old picture frame with broken glass. The picture had faded with time.

Grace wanted to look over the front of the boat, which was on its side, so she swam around to the front. The cabin was covered with moss and other ocean plants. The masts had broken, and a few pieces of them stuck out here and there. Pieces of rope were tied to different parts of the boat, seemingly in tangles.

But there wasn't much to see. Grace was pretty sure there wouldn't be much around the boat either.

Sam, on the other hand, was scanning every square inch. He was even sweeping dust and moss off of things. He had already found a couple coins this way. They were ordinary coins though, nothing incredible.

Grace swam in through the hole in the boat. It was dark in there, and several fish swam away when she entered. She turned on the light above her mask. Inside, there were broken shelves and chairs. It was a mess.

By the way it looked, Grace guessed that the boat had been lifted by a tidal wave and dropped on a large boulder. Then the boat had filled with water, and it had sunk. She wondered if everyone had made it out safely or, she shuddered, if someone had died.

Being honest with herself, Grace could sense that something horrible had happened there. The way everything was torn apart and thrown around seemed to whisper a chill that haunted the place. Grace looked at the hatch, which was thrust open. In her mind, she could almost hear screams as the victims of the sinking boat struggled to get away.

It was almost as if the waves that blurred the sunlight from the surface created an image before her. She could see the boat sinking in her mind, and she could hear the calls for help. Grace found a boot and she almost screamed.

The whole boat seemed to grow with terror in Grace's mind. She decided it was time to go.

Spinning around, she hit the side of the open hatch. The impact from the hit sent her falling towards the bottom of the ship. Her head hit the ground – hard. For a moment, her vision blacked out.

But when her vision cleared, her eyes were set upon something. It glimmered in the dim light, shimmering in the movement of the water. Grace swam towards it, to get a better look. It was mostly covered with sand, but when Grace had hit the side of the boat, it had disturbed the debris that had settled on the ocean floor. And somehow, this thing had appeared where it hadn't been visible before.

Grace reached down carefully. Reaching for the object, she realized how small it was. With her large gloves, she could barely grasp it, but with effort, she was able to, and when she did, she held it out so she could see it clearly.

To her astonishment, it was the most unlikely item she had expected to find. In her fingertips, she held a long, gold chain. Dangling from it was a locket. It was shaped like a heart – unharmed by the watery grave where it had waited for all of these years.

Suddenly, Grace felt as if she was holding a piece of history – a piece of a story that was forgotten. But Grace wasn't sure if she wanted to know more about the history of this boat and those who had been doomed to its fate.

Though she wanted to drop the chain and forget about it, she felt almost as if the locket had found her. If she hadn't hit the side of the boat, she would have never found it; if it hadn't shone in the sunlight, she wouldn't have found it either.

It was almost as if the locket had been handed to her, like an unseen force had helped her fall in just the right direction so that it would be uncovered, and so that she would find it.

The locket had come to her for a reason, and Grace knew it.

...

She had been standing there for a while, just holding the locket and staring. By the time she realized that she was in a sort of trance, Sam was standing behind her. He was as amazed as she was. They both knew the same thing – this locket was what they had come for.

...

Back on the boat, speeding towards shore, Sam and Grace looked at the locket.

"Do you think there's anything inside it?" Grace asked.

Sam shrugged. "It doesn't seem like anything would be, after that long."

There was an initial etched on the front. It was a C – just a C. Grace ran her fingers over the locket, feeling every detail on its face. She tried to imagine the owner of the locket. Had this person lived, or had she perished in the shipwreck? It was more than Grace could tell.

"Why don't you open it?" Sam spoke softly.

Grace nodded and took a deep breath. She desperately wanted something to be inside, but at the same time, she didn't want anything to be there. She wanted to know who had owned the necklace, but she was afraid that it would lead to a terrible truth – perhaps a painful story, a story that included death.

With her fingernails, she carefully undid the snap that held the two hearts together. She took another deep breath before opening it, glancing up at Sam for reassurance.

He nodded impatiently.

Grace opened the locket slowly. When the light fell upon the inside, to her amazement, two pictures had remained. The pictures had somehow survived the shipwreck and their years underwater. It seemed impossible to Grace for them to have been preserved like this, but at the same time, it made sense. With these pictures, a story was told. Though the facts weren't for sure, a story lay before Sam and Grace.

On one side of the locket was the picture of a girl. "She was beautiful," Grace noted. Her chin was small and delicate, and on her face was a gentle smile. She had to be in her early twenties or late teens. Her hair was wound up around her head in the fashion of the time period. Grace guessed it was sometime late in the Edwardian era.

To Grace, it seemed as if she knew this woman, and she felt a connection with her, though she didn't understand why or how. The curve of her chin and slope of her nose were all too familiar, and the familiarity made everything even queerer.

On the other side of the locket was the picture of a young man. He was dressed in a suit of the era. He wasn't really smiling, but his eyes held a playful gleam, one of adventure and excitement. He wore a dark, broad-brimmed hat pulled down, nearly to his eyebrows.

Questions were swelling in Grace's mind. Who were these people? And what had happened to them? Were they still alive? Did Grace, in fact know them, or one of them?

Sam was obviously equally puzzled. "They both seem so familiar to me. It's crazy how familiar they are. I feel like I should know who both of them are... but I don't remember."

Grace didn't seem to recognize the lad as much as she recognized the girl, but they did both seem familiar.

They stared for a long, long time, not speaking much – just looking. Soon they reached the dock by the lighthouse, and Grace and Sam climbed out.

"Thank you, Grey, for taking us," Sam said. "You have been a big help."

"Good luck with your searches, friend." Grey shook Sam's hand in a firm, sailor's grip.

Then he turned to Grace and touched the brim of his hat, "Nice to meet you, Miss Grace," he said. "I hope we will see each other again – soon."

Grace nodded. "We will." She smiled and waved as Grey turned the boat and sailed away. Then she realized it would be a good time to head home. "I'd better get going, before my aunt goes searching for me again," she explained as she gathered her things.

"I'll meet you tomorrow?" Sam asked hopefully.

Grace paused a moment, thinking. It would probably seem less suspicious to her aunt if she spent a day at home again. "Maybe I had better stay home tomorrow – to keep my aunt from getting suspicious."

"I wish your aunt wasn't against us. She hasn't met me. Why can't she just give me a chance?" Sam's face flushed in his frustration.

Grace shrugged. "I don't think it's you – I think it's your uncle. She doesn't trust him for some reason."

"Buy why? He wouldn't do a thing. He's just a nice old man, and the only family I've got," Sam spoke wistfully.

"I don't get it either, but we'll get to the bottom of it, sooner or later," Grace said.

"All right," Sam said. "Then if you don't come tomorrow, you have to come the day after that –promise?"

Grace took a deep breath before answering. "I will see what I can do. If I can, then I will."

"And then we can try to figure out more about the locket..." Sam encouraged.

"And the pocket watch..." Grace reminded him.

"Right," Sam said.

And with that, Grace took her picnic basket and ran back up the hill. She was as happy as a lark. With the locket around her neck, she almost felt like singing. She was so excited about solving the mystery of the locket, and it seemed to her like there was something important about to happen. She couldn't help but be happy.

When she reached the sagging gate however, she had another thought and that had to do with her hair. That morning it had been brushed neatly, but now, it was unkempt from getting wet and then drying again.

It would take a whole lot of scheming to keep her aunt from noticing it, and a whole lot more to keep her from worrying.

THE LETTER

When Grace got home, she hurried through the kitchen and up to her room as quickly as she could. Amazingly, her aunt wasn't around, so everything was all right.

Inside her room, Grace made sure to fix her hair and be ready for dinner, or at least, ready to run into her aunt again.

But then, she had extra time before dinner, so she got out her diary again. This time, though, Grace thought it would be pleasant to write outside, so she took the little book downstairs with her.

In her aunt's backyard, which Grace hadn't seen anything of yet, there was a cobblestone path. It wasn't very long, but there were flowerbeds and gardens on either side of it. At the end of the path, there was a bench-swing. It hung underneath a large tree, with rods going up on either side that acted like a trellis. Climbing roses were wrapped around the rods, and the leaves and blossoms shaded the bench from direct sunlight.

Grace sat down on the bench and swung back and forth a little. The scent of the roses was so strong and sweet. She closed her eyes to breathe it in. This would be her new hideaway.

And then she opened her book and began to write.

...

It hadn't been long since Grey left, that Sam's uncle returned. He was smiling broadly—secrets sparkling from his eyes. But though Sam wanted to ask why, he didn't. He knew that if he was meant to know, his uncle would tell him. This was the way that they gave each other space.

"You were gone early this morning," his uncle commented.

"Ya, I had a lot to do..." Sam admitted.

"I saw Grey leaving here."

"He took me and—um... him... on a boat ride," Sam stuttered.

"I see," His uncle said. "I also saw the three of you out on the water."

"Oh. You did?"

His uncle nodded.

"I had to. And Grace wanted to come, so..." Sam broke off, not knowing what excuses to add.

"I don't know what her aunt will say about it, but things might get bad pretty fast."

Sam expected the scolding to get worse, but it didn't. His uncle was in too good of a mood to have it changed, and Sam even saw a slight smile under his uncle's gray beard. It was almost like he agreed and understood somehow.

But Sam wasn't going to spend his thinking time trying to figure his uncle out. There were other times for that. Instead, Sam went up to his room. He needed to add everything they had found on their diving trip to his book.

In his room, with his drawer open and the map strewn across the floor, Sam carefully started drawing dots in the area where the shipwreck was. He had already drawn a large circle with pencil to show where the ship was, but now he was plotting out all of the objects that they had found. There was a yellow dot for the picture frame, green dots for the coins, purple dots for the bottles he had picked up, and then one red dot – for the locket.

Sam would have liked to have 'borrowed' the locket, but Grace wouldn't let him, so he had to try his best to remember it as he drew in his book. He knew it was heart-shaped, and he knew there were pictures inside, and there was a smaller design of a heart on the front. There was a curvy line that ran around the whole thing, and then there was the 'C' on the front.

Sam drew one angle of the locket from the outside, sort of like it was open and you were looking at it from behind. Then he drew the inside. It was difficult to draw the people in the pictures, but when Sam was finished, they amazed him. Somehow he had been able to capture a little bit of the familiar traits in both pictures. This made him bristle because it really showed how well he knew the faces.

...

The next morning was overcast. When Sam woke up, he couldn't think of a good reason to get up—there were no places he planned to hunt for things, and Grace wasn't coming. There weren't even any scheduled ocean liners to be arriving.

So, weighing out the balance of everything, Sam decided that it would be all right if he slept a little longer.

...

Grace, on the other hand, was up bright and early. She felt good this morning. Sam wasn't trying to get her to do anything, and she didn't have to try to sneak past her aunt. She was perfectly relaxed. Her aunt noticed her change in mood as well. "Good morning, Grace. You're up bright and early this morning," she said.

"Ya," Grace said. She sat down and served herself a bowl of hot cereal.

"Do you have special plans for today?" her aunt asked.

"...Not really," Grace answered.

"Well... I would have guessed that you had plans for the day with how early you got up."

Grace laughed. "Well, I don't."

Her aunt suddenly felt as if it was her responsibility to think of something for Grace to do. "Well... today is laundry day."

Suddenly Grace's carelessness disappeared. "Laundry day?" Her heart began to race, and her mind started spinning. Her clothes held all of the evidence that her aunt needed. Grace had said that she was going on a picnic. Where, then, would she get three-days worth of clothes that were all covered in sand?

"I was going to have to get your laundry out of your room myself, but..."

"Oh no, Clarenne. I wouldn't let you do that." Grace was thinking fast. "I mean, well I always do my laundry myself."

"Oh, you do?" Clarenne sounded pleased.

"Yep."

"I never would have guessed."

Grace shrugged. "It's kind of a fad of mine."

"I see." Her aunt was surprised into silence for a moment. "Oh," she said at last. "We don't have any washing machines in the house, so I usually go to the launders. There's a little laundry shop in town, where you can wash your laundry."

"Sounds great to me. Really, I thought you were going to say that you liked to scrub them by hand, and then string them out to dry," Grace said with a laugh of forced humor.

"Oh," her aunt chuckled comfortingly. "I am somewhat old-fashioned, but not that old-fashioned. Some things you just have to upgrade."

"So, when are we going?" Grace was relieved. For one, she would get to take care of her laundry herself, and second, she could spend the whole day with her aunt—which she thought would be good for both herself and her aunt.

...

By the time Sam got up, it was already past midmorning. and when he went downstairs, it was dark and all of the food had been cleaned up. But Sam didn't mind this. He got out a box of cold cereal and filled a bowl. He added milk, and sat down on one of the stools at the kitchen table.

He ate in silence, crouched over his bowl. His mind felt numb and empty. No thoughts or feelings... Sam was still sort of tired, and it didn't seem like there was anything important to think about.

If Sam had been more observant, he would have noticed the note that was stuck to the fridge. Its contents were worth thinking about, but Sam hadn't seen it, and he didn't even suspect there being a note like that.

From where he sat, Sam should have noticed that his uncle's boots and hooded raincoat were both missing, along with his fishing pole and tackle box. Sam should have noticed these things because he was such an observant person, but today he didn't.

Sam should have also noticed the cloud-filled sky, like Grace had, but he hadn't even noticed that yet. He only noticed the contents of his cereal bowl, and that he was apparently alone in the lighthouse. This meant he had a nice, long day ahead of him.

When he had finished eating, Sam figured this would be a good time to do the dishes. They were starting to build up in the kitchen, and though they weren't exactly his chores, he did them every now and then, just to help his uncle out.

...

On their way back from the launders a couple hours later, a light sprinkling began covering the windshield. Grace and her aunt laughed and chatted in the car. Grace had never seen Clarenne this out of herself. Somehow, having someone with her, she had been able to break out of her usual self, and she was laughing like a kid again.

"... I really thought that's what old people did. Honest," Grace insisted.

"I do not sit around and knit," her aunt was laughing tears now. "That's for old fogies."

"Then what do you do all day?" Grace questioned.

"There are lots of things to do. I have to go shopping, and I have to clean the house... And then I have to prepare the meals, wash the dishes, and do the laundry. There are always things to do, but when I do get everything done, I like to read."

"So you're not old then, even though you're basically eighty?"

"No, I'm not old," her aunt said with decision.

"Then what classifies an old person?" Grace was serious.

Her aunt shrugged. "I'm not sure, but it must have to do with how old you feel. And I don't feel old. You won't find me sitting around in an old-folks home any time soon. I guess I'm just young at heart," she smiled, "especially when you're around like this!"

By now the car was parked in front of the house, and Clarenne reached to tickle Grace's neck.

Grace shrieked. "Don't do that. It's not fair."

Clarenne was laughing uncontrollably now. "I haven't tickled anyone in a long time." Then she was lost in another fit of giggles.

"Most people aren't ticklish there, but I am," Grace was still laughing.

"My sister was, too." For a minute Clarenne was silent. "You know? I really miss her. Nothing has been the same since... since..."

Grace could see the sadness creeping back into her aunt's eyes. All of the teasing and happiness was disappearing as she gazed out at the ocean again.

"But now things are different," Grace said suddenly. "Why don't we get the laundry out of the car? Then we can do something else."

"That sounds good, Grace. Thank you," her aunt smiled, but she still had pain in her eyes.

...

When Sam had finished the dishes, he went back up the stairs to his room. The note sat untouched and unread. Sam hadn't noticed that the rain had picked up a little. Even though it had been a while since there had been a storm on the island, Sam didn't notice.

Really, if he had read the note, he would have done things differently...

GONE

It wasn't until that evening when Sam began to worry about his uncle. He hadn't come for dinner. In fact, Sam hadn't seen him at all that day, and it all seemed very strange to him. He was sure that there had been something going on with his uncle the day before, but he hadn't anticipated a disappearance like this.

When Sam went to the fridge for dinner, he noticed the message on the fridge. Taking it down, he read it. There were only a few short phrases scrawled across the page:

Sam,

I have gone fishing. I've been in need of a break from the island for a while.

Everything has been getting harder to cope with. I hope you understand. I had planned to tell you in person, but I couldn't wait.

I don't know how long I will be gone. Perhaps a couple of days. Keep the lighthouse burning brightly in my absence – you know how.

And don't worry about me.

Your Uncle,
E. Warner

It all seemed a little queer to Sam, but knowing where his uncle was soothed his worries for a while. Besides, his uncle said not to worry, so Sam wouldn't. He didn't mind keeping the lighthouse to himself for a couple of days, so he just made himself a couple peanut butter sandwiches for dinner.

...

That night, though, he could hear gentle rain outside his bedroom window. It seemed somehow treacherous, knowing that his uncle wasn't around. Again he remembered the last line of the letter telling him not to worry. So, again, he pushed the thoughts from his mind. Everything was all right, and would be all right.

Tomorrow Grace would be coming, and that was something to look forward to, though if it was stormy, Sam didn't know what they would do.

...

The next morning Grace woke up indecently early. Getting away from the house this time, she knew, would be particularly hard, so she decided she had better do it before her aunt was awake. Because it was stormy outside, Grace was having a hard time thinking of an excuse to tell her aunt. She hoped that just leaving early would work.

As quiet as a mouse, Grace slipped down the stairs and into the kitchen. There was an umbrella in the closet where the coats were hung. Grace took a jacket as well because it was kind of chilly outside.

When Grace opened the front door, she realized how dark it was. With the gray clouds and the rain, everything was darker than it should be. Grace was afraid for a moment, but she knew this was her only chance to get away from the house, so she took it. She carried a flashlight hoping that it would help her find her way.

On the porch of the house, she opened the umbrella and began making her way down the drive in front of the house. In the dark and the rain, Grace's flashlight cast long beams of light across the land beyond. The water droplets that fell caught the light and shimmered back.

Everything was quiet outside, except for the constant hush of the rain hitting the ground and the leaves on the trees. It was a gentle rain, though it fell evenly. Grace decided to take her time, especially as she didn't want to arrive at the lighthouse too early.

In the silence of her own thoughts, Grace followed the road. She breathed in the smell of the ozone from the lightning, enjoying how everything smelt damp, almost raw. She could smell the mud and the grass. It was a comfortable scent. Grace liked going out in the rain, though she hadn't been able to do it frequently.

...

By the time she reached the sagging gate, the sky was beginning to get lighter. She hadn't noticed it, as the light had grown so gradually it kind of snuck up on her, but when she saw the gate, she realized that it was brighter now, so she put the flashlight away.

Climbing over the gate was more difficult, as it was covered with rain droplets. Grace took more time to climb over – being sure not to slip. She had to close the umbrella to free up her hands, and the rain felt good as it fell on her face for a moment.

Then she opened the umbrella back up and continued on down the trail towards the lighthouse. There were strong winds that seemed to push her forward at times, but then they would turn around and push against her.

Grace kept walking, knowing that it wouldn't be long before she arrived at the lighthouse. It wasn't until then that a thought crossed her mind. What if the lighthouse keeper was there? Grace knew Sam, and she trusted him. Her aunt didn't know Sam, so Grace felt like she could still give him a chance, but as far as the lighthouse keeper went, Grace didn't know him at all, except for how her aunt felt about him, and it was enough to make her shiver. What kind of person had inspired such intense feelings of dislike in her aunt?

Then and there she almost turned around and walked all of the way back home. It was her knowledge of Sam that finally reassured her. She knew, deep down inside with a feeling that she couldn't explain, that she could trust Sam. He would make sure that everything was all right.

...

By now she could see the lighthouse ahead of her. Now that it was getting lighter, she could see a blanket of fog that rose from the ocean, and the lighthouse shone a bright, steady light in all directions.

This was the closest Grace had been to the lighthouse while it was on, and it was an incredible sight. She could almost feel warmth radiating from it. She felt as if she was a lost ship in a storm, and now she could see the lighthouse, and it was leading her on.

...

Sam had been up since dawn as well, except he was watching the rain from the safety of the lighthouse Watch. The raindrops painted patterns on the windows that surrounded him, blurring his view of the world beyond, but even then, he watched.

Though he didn't want to admit it, he was just a little worried. He was worried about his uncle, and he was worried about Grace. He hoped that she would still be able to come. If his uncle didn't show up, it would at least make it easier for him to tell someone about his uncle leaving.

From the Watch in the lighthouse, Sam could see the red umbrella, and he knew right away that it was Grace. The sight made him forget his worries.

...

Grace was looking up at the glorious light. Just then, the light in the watch of the lighthouse blinked off, then back on again. It did this three times. Grace wondered about it at first, but then she realized that it was a signal. Sam was up in the Watch, and he had seen her.

...

By the time Grace reached the door to the lighthouse, Sam had gone down all of the stairs that led up to the Watch. Grace reached to knock just as Sam threw the door open.

"You made it," he said.

"Yeah, I had to leave early. I'm sure my aunt would get really suspicious if she saw me going out in the rain."

Sam shrugged. "Have you eaten breakfast yet?"

Grace avoided the question. "I'm fine."

"Well I was just about to make breakfast." Grace followed him into the kitchen. "My uncle left yesterday. He went on a fishing trip."

"In the storm? Isn't that dangerous?"

Sam shrugged again. "I don't know. He said not to worry about him... in this letter that I found." Sam pulled the letter out of his pocket and let her read it.

"You mean he didn't tell you?"

"No, he just left the message. I didn't see it until late evening yesterday... I really don't know why he would go off in a storm..." Grace could see Sam's worry before he quickly changed the subject. "The letter says not to worry about him, so I won't."

Grace nodded. "Unless he takes too long to come back..."

Sam agreed and changed the subject again. "Breakfast. Do you want anything? We could make omelets or something."

...

It didn't take Grace long to realize that she was making the omelets and Sam was helping. He showed her where everything was, and he helped cut up the vegetables and crack the eggs.

Pretty soon, the kitchen smelled wonderful. Sam was glad that Grace hadn't eaten breakfast before. It had been like forever since he'd had an omelet. As he watched her fold in the edges of the omelet, he realized that Grace was an experienced cook.

They both sat on stools at the kitchen table, with their sizzling omelets before them.

Then Sam squirted ketchup all over his.

"Wow," Grace said.

"Ketchup is good on everything," Sam told her.

When breakfast was finished, Grace insisted that they do the dishes. She didn't like the feeling of having dirty dishes lingering around the kitchen counters. Besides, she reasoned that it wouldn't take long, so Sam gave in.

"So... now what?" Grace asked, as Sam put the last dish in the cupboard and turned around.

"I'm not really sure..." he said. "It wasn't supposed to be rainy today."

"What? You don't have anything to do, and I came all of the way over here? For no reason?" Grace teased.

"Wait... there's a reason. I mean, we can try to figure out more about the locket."

Grace shrugged. "What would we figure out? We don't know who the people are. So..."

"Well, what else could we do?" Sam asked.

"I don't know." Grace thought for a minute. Rainy days really were dull, especially, Grace thought, when you have a mystery that needs to be solved. She knew she shouldn't really be going anywhere outside right now, so they wouldn't be able to look for clues, and there wasn't a very good way to look people up by their pictures anyway... She thought about the police. Did they have a way to figure out who people from long ago were, just by looking at their pictures? It seemed hopeless, and besides, the police probably wouldn't even want to help two kids find the identity of some old locket – there was no reason for it.

"Well..." Grace was stalling. There had to be something that they could do, even though they had to stay inside. For crying out loud, she was in the lighthouse. Though the locket seemed to be somehow related to that mystery she had felt when she had first seen the lighthouse, it seemed like there was something more.

"Aren't there more places in the lighthouse? Like any hiding places or something? What if there's something hidden in the lighthouse that could give us a clue," Grace spoke the thoughts as they burst into her mind.

It sounded somewhat reasonable to Sam, though at the same time it sounded kind of dull. He had lived in the lighthouse basically all his life. There wasn't anything extra-special about it, or at least, he had never thought of it being special just because he was used to it.

"I don't know," he said.

"What about an attic... or a basement?"

"There isn't exactly an attic. There's a metal roof with a lightning rod on it, but it's not exactly the smartest place to be in a storm."

Too bad, Grace thought.

"But there is a basement. I haven't really gone down there. I used to be scared of it, but it's just a dirty storage area..." Sam was saying, but Grace was excited.

"It's a perfect place for history and clues to be hiding. Haven't you ever heard of those stories where they find an heirloom or something in the cellar? Who knows what could be down there? There could be things that have been passed down for centuries."

...

"Are you really sure this is a great idea?" Sam said from behind.

Grace was in the lead. The basement door was located in the floor of a utility closet, and it had been difficult to open. But now that it was open, Grace could see cement steps that led into the darkness. Grace had her flashlight, and she had it on. She scanned the room from one side to the next as she descended carefully down the filthy stairs.

"Really, I'm sure there are other things we could do," Sam tried again.

Grace shone the flashlight in Sam's direction.

"Not in my face..." Sam said.

Grace pointed the flashlight at the ceiling. "If you're so scared, you can just wait up there, but I think there's something down here that can help us."

"How?"

"I don't know. Don't you ever just get gut-feelings?"

Sam shrugged. "Not usually."

"Whatever." Grace kept on taking the stairs. She was alert and careful, but she wasn't scared like Sam was. Obviously he had come in here once and really freaked out about something. She smiled imagining Sam as a small boy.

There were cobwebs all over the place. They hung thick from the ceiling. Grace carefully ducked underneath them. Sam, being taller, walked right into one. The web covered his face, and he coughed and spit as he tried to get it off. "Yuck! I hate spider webs."

Grace couldn't help but snicker a little.

Just a few steps from the bottom of the staircase, there was a light switch on the wall. It had a fancy cover, though it was terribly dirty and the metal that had once been shiny was corroding now.

Grace carefully flipped the switch.

The room lit up, though it wasn't a lot of light. There was a bulb that hung from the ceiling by a chain. It was so dusty that its light was dimmed, and it was so old that it made the room look orange.

The basement was actually a pretty large room, but it was crammed so full of junk that it seemed very small. There were several shelves that lined the walls, and there was an assortment of boxes everywhere. Everything was covered in a fine layer of dust.

There was furniture, some of it was broken and some was old and had just been replaced. Chairs were stacked on top of each other – their backs covered with webs. There was a bed leaning up against the wall. Its mattress was in front of it, and springs jutted out of the holes in it. Grace imagined someone had done some serious jumping on that mattress.

In a corner of the room, there was an old mirror. There were two skinny mirrors on either side that could be hinged forward and back, and in the middle was a chest of sorts. It was a small box, angled down with a lid that hinged up. It was attached to the base of the mirror. The mirror's frame was an off-white shade. The poor mirror was so dusty it almost couldn't reflect. There were streaks on it, like someone had once wiped off the dust, but more dust had collected on it since then.

Over all, everything looked like junk. There were old pots and dishes. Sam opened a box and found a couple pieces of fancy china. The dishes were chipped on the edges, and the paint that must have looked bright at first, was now faded with age.

"See what I mean?" Sam said. "It's all junk."

"But it's not just any ordinary junk. Don't you get it? This is the past, the history of the lighthouse. This stuff was new... but then it was used. Every spring bent out of shape or broken chair has a story. We might not know the story, but that doesn't mean that there isn't a story."

Grace was right, and her words made Sam look around the room with new eyes. He'd never thought of the junk in the cellar like this before.

"You mean there could be something down here that could have belonged to the person who had the locket?" Sam asked.

Grace nodded. "Either that or maybe something that has to do with the pocket watch. Who would lose something in this part of the island? I mean, there's nothing out here but the lighthouse."

"Right – so the locket must have belonged to someone who lived at the lighthouse..." Sam started.

"Or a friend of someone who lived at the lighthouse," Grace finished.

And suddenly Sam was going through all of the boxes. He was going to be as thorough as he was around the ship wreckage, but Grace's plan went on further than what she had explained. She reasoned that she might possibly be able to find a portrait of one of the people whose pictures she had found in the locket.

Within moments, she had discovered what she had been looking for – a pile of old picture frames with pictures inside. They were standing against the wall, tucked away in a corner. Some of the frames were really big, while others were small. The larger the frames were, the fancier they seemed to be. There were floral designs carved into them and fancy curves, but most of the frames were broken in the corners, or they were missing the glass that went with them.

There were several large pieces of broken glass. Grace was careful not to get cut as she looked through the frames. It wasn't just a pile of frames. There were pictures mixed in as well. Grace guessed that either the pictures had just faded and been re-placed, or the frames had broken and never been fixed.

At any rate they had all ended up in a tangled mess.

Grace stopped for a moment and observed a painting of the lighthouse. It was beautiful. The detail was fine to a point. It portrayed the lighthouse in a storm, from the helm of a boat. You could see the steering wheel of the boat, and the lighthouse was in the distance. Waves rose up around the boat, trying, it seemed, to swallow it whole. But the picture gave the clear impression that the captain wasn't giving up and that the lighthouse gave him hope that he would make it to the shore.

There were other paintings, too. Some of the styles were odd. Grace understood why they would be down here instead of hanging in the halls. There was a picture of the moon over the ocean, the whole thing was a soft blue with the moon being a bright white. This picture, though, had a tear in the corner... And then there was a painting of a warm, summer day with the view of the ocean through a glade of trees. It was a view similar to the one Grace had seen when she had first gone to the beach.

Near the very back of the pile, there was a portrait. It was a painting that had been painted with rough strokes, but still fine – evidentially painted in the style of the era.

When Grace saw it, she gasped.

"Sam... Sam, you have to see this!" she stammered.

THE FORGOTTEN PORTRAIT

For some unexplainable reason, seeing this painting made Grace emotional. Pieces were falling together in her mind, and they were falling so quickly that she had no time to completely understand. The picture was unharmed, pristine in every way. Why would this picture be in the basement?

Suddenly it all made sense. They had put this picture here for the same reason that Grace had hidden the picture of her Father and Mother. She couldn't stand to look at it because it made her miss them more than she could express.

It pricked that pain that lay deep inside her heart, the one that couldn't heal. That part was missing, and it wouldn't ever come back, and so she had hidden the picture. Not because she wanted to forget her parents, but so that she could somehow go on... without them.

Sam was at her side, "What's wrong?" He looked from her tears to the painting.

When he saw the painting, he recognized it. It was a painting of the same girl in the locket. It had the same small lips and playful eyes, but this time, with a picture large enough to see all of the detail, he saw the locket that she wore, the locket in the shape of a heart with a 'C' in the middle.

...

It took Grace a while to get her composure back. She knew somehow, she just knew that this girl had died. She had died in the shipwreck, and now Grace wasn't sure if she wanted to know any more. She could feel herself wanting to bury the past, just like she was trying to bury her own past.

Sam had pulled the picture from the pile and had set it against the wall. Grace crouched in a corner, sobbing endless tears.

Sam couldn't understand why she was crying, and really, he didn't know how it felt to have his parents die. He had never known his parents. He didn't even know who they were, and his uncle had always been there for him. He hadn't lost anyone.

But Grace was still trying to heal, and it seemed now as if someone else, another someone, had died. Poor Sam didn't know how to comfort her, and so he just sat there and waited awhile. It hurt him to watch what she was going through, and he wished that somehow he could take away the pain, or that he could go through some of it for her.

When her tears were all cried, Grace sniffled and said, "Sam, let's turn the picture around. It might say who the painting is of on the back."

"Are you okay with all of this, Grace?" Sam was still concerned.

"I'm fine. Really. It's just that there are a lot of things that I'm trying to deal with right now, but there's no point in crying. Crying never does anyone any good." Grace spoke as if she was trying to convince herself.

She got up, and the two of them carefully turned the frame around. There wasn't anything on the back of the frame, except for a hook to mount it on the wall.

"Darn," Grace said.

But Sam didn't give up so easily. "There might be something behind the back of the frame," he suggested. Then he laid the picture on its face and carefully pried up the bent staples that held the back of the frame on. Grace helped him lift it off when he was done.

Sure enough, there on the back of the canvas was a piece of paper. It was weathered and so old it had turned yellow. The tape that had been used to secure it had turned brown, and it had lost most of its stick. But there were words that still showed up distinctly. Sam carefully removed the page and read its contents aloud:

Your moveable light,
That shines in the night,
Showing the way
Through darkened day...
That little flame,
Beneath its blaze,
You'll find my name...

—Charlotte

"That makes no sense," Grace retorted.

"At least now we know her name," Sam said.

"But what is the rest of the message saying?" Grace argued.

"It seems like it's some sort of clue," Sam said wistfully.

"Why would a riddle be written on the back of a picture, though?" Grace still didn't agree.

"Maybe it was supposed to be found," Sam suggested.

And then a shiver ran down Grace's spine. Was this the mystery she had felt from the ocean liner when she had first seen the lighthouse? She changed her tone, "Okay, what's a moveable light?"

"Well, the light in the lighthouse can't be moved..." Sam thought for a moment. "A light that can be moved... it could be like a flashlight or something?"

"That seems right; flashlights show the way when it's dark, but what about the flame? Flashlights don't really have a flame," Grace pointed out.

"They have light bulbs, but you're right, that's different... and I think it's the wrong time period, too. I mean, were flashlights around when this was written?" Sam disagreed with his own idea.

"Probably not," Grace agreed. "But then what would they have used instead?"

"A candle?"

"That's got to be it," Grace said getting up. "Where do you keep candles?"

"Um, there's a cupboard in the kitchen where we have matches and stuff. We don't usually use them, though," Sam didn't sound convinced.

"That should mean that the candle we need is still there," Grace said.

...

In the kitchen, they looked through all of the candles in the cupboard. There weren't very many in the cupboard, so it didn't take long, but when they were finished, they were both disappointed. They had found nothing, not a single clue.

"Well, it looks like that riddle led us on a wild goose chase," Sam admitted.

"We can't give up yet," Grace said. "That message must have meant something."

"But what? Maybe there was a clue on a candle, and the candle was used up a long time ago," Sam said.

Grace thought about it. She knew Sam was right. Candles were so small, and they burned down so quickly. It was foolish to think that a candle would still be around after so many years, but maybe the clue wasn't talking about a candle? Maybe it was telling about something else entirely.

"Well, if it's not a candle what else could it be?" Grace asked.

"I don't know," Sam said with a careless shrug. "Grace, just give it up... it's impossible. The clues are too old anyway."

"A lantern! It's talking about a lantern! Doesn't that make more sense? I mean, how in the world could a name be on a candle?" Grace was nearly shouting in her excitement.

Grace had guessed that it was a lantern, but when she had said the words, Sam knew she was right. And he knew more than that. He knew exactly which lantern it was talking about.

"Hey, I know where it is!" Sam said proudly.

"Where?" Grace's eyes were round in anticipation.

"My uncle has a lantern. It's in his room and he always uses it. For some reason he's never replaced it with a flashlight. I could never figure out why, but I guess it's been passed down or something."

"That must be it!" Grace said, clapping her hands together.

"He even told me it had a name," Sam continued.

"The lantern has a name?" Grace was surprised.

"Yeah... it's Lottie."

THE MAP

"I don't get it. Lottie?" Grace was confused.

"Don't you see? Lottie is a nickname for Charlotte," Sam explained.

"So the lantern was named after her?" Grace wondered.

"Or it was named before her. Remember, it's really old?" Sam reminded.

"You're right, but how would she know about the lantern? And who's the guy in the other picture?" Grace asked.

Sam shrugged, leading Grace through the lighthouse. His uncle's room was on the far side of the building. This side of the lighthouse hadn't been included in Grace's original tour.

"Will we get in trouble for going in here?" Grace asked.

"He wouldn't mind. We're just looking at the lantern," Sam reassured.

The room was somewhat tidy; at least the covers on the bed had been pulled up. There wasn't much more in the room besides the bed. A window was at one side of the room, and there was a bookshelf with a few books. There was a lamp with a blue shade. It matched the color of the coverlet on the bed, and the shades at the window.

Beside the window, hanging on a hook, was the lantern "Lottie". Sam carefully took the lantern down. "So, what do we do with it?" he asked.

"The riddle said it's beneath the flame," Grace said.

They looked at the lantern carefully, and there was a ring that went around the wick of the lantern. The oil was beneath it, and the bottle unscrewed. Carefully, Sam removed the bottle of oil. Nothing, but there was a silver ring that encased the wick. This had a seam in the middle.

Taking a deep breath, Sam tried to unscrew the ring. It spun with a little effort. Obviously this wasn't done frequently, and it probably wasn't supposed to be done. Someone could refuel the lantern without ever unscrewing the ring.

With the outside part of the ring off, there was a tiny compartment. It was just big enough to fit a skinny piece of paper, which was folded and wrapped around the ring. It fell to the floor when the outer ring was removed.

Grace picked it up and opened it. She recognized the handwriting immediately. It had the same flourishes, but it wasn't a clue. It was a list:

1. Mackinac Lighthouse

2. Hoover Bridge

3. Crooked Neck Stream

4. Grey's Pier

5. *Donovan Park*

6. *Corner Café*

7. *Compass Star*

8. *King Fischer's General Store*

9. *Skeleton Rock*

10. *Grand Hotel*

11. *Dockery School*

For a moment they both puzzled over the list.

"Are these places?" Grace asked at last.

"Ya," Sam said.

"Are we supposed to find clues in all of these places?" Grace wondered.

Sam shrugged. "I guess. Except, I don't know where Compass Star is."

"Maybe we could look it up in the phone book?" mentioned Grace.

"Or we could just look on the map that's in the library," Sam suggested.

Grace remembered the map from the tour Sam had given. It seemed like a good idea to look at the map, especially because it was rainy outside and not a good day to be looking for clues all over town. Besides, Grace had no idea how they would get all around the city without her aunt finding out. That would be a challenge in and of itself.

They carefully put the lantern back together and hung it back in its place on the hook beside the window. Then they went to find the map.

...

In the library, they both began searching the map for Compass Star. Sam started on the left, and Grace took the right. It didn't make sense to her why there would be a place called Compass Star, but she looked anyway. Meanwhile, in her head, she was trying to remember what a Compass Star was. It sounded like something that had to do with directions, or maybe with maps.

And then she figured it out. There on the right side of the map, in the bottom corner, was a "compass star". In really small writing was the letter "S" tucked away in one of the corners of the star.

"Sam, look!" she yelled. She pointed out the "S" for Sam to see. "I think there are letters hidden in all of these places?" Grace explained.

Soon they had a notebook with lines numbered from one to eleven. On number seven, they wrote the letter "S". Sam pointed out the lighthouse on the map. There they found the letter "C". Grace thought it was somehow significant. It seemed like there were lots of things with the letter "C".

Grace didn't know where Hoover Bridge was, but Sam pointed it out, and soon they had found the letter "R". Crooked Neck Stream was just a little stream that ran through the city. It passed nearby Grace's home. There was a bend in the stream with the letter "E" next to it.

Grey's Pier, of course, was where Grey would sell and rent boats, and it was also where Grace had first arrived on the island. There Sam found an "A". Grace found Donovan Park all by herself, but finding the letter was harder. She finally found a letter "K" next to the gazebo. The Corner Café was a little coffee shop in the middle of the city, and it had the letter "Y".

Here they stopped and looked at their list. The letters formed the word: C-R-E-A-K-Y. It didn't make a lot of sense yet, so they kept going.

Compass Star, of course, had the letter "S". Then King Fischer's General Store had a letter "T" right in the middle of the parking lot. Sam had to point out where Skeleton Rock was. "It's kind of a funny place. I mean, they're just rocks out in the water, next to the cliffs," Sam explained.

Grace understood why it was called Skeleton Rock. It was a strange shape, and it looked strangely similar to a skull. There was another letter "A" next to it. The Grand Hotel was the biggest, fanciest hotel on the island. It was where all of the tourists would get rooms, or at least all of the rich tourists. There was a letter "I" next to it.

And Dockery School, the only High School on the whole island, had another "R". It was where Sam went to school, and Grace guessed she would be going there as soon as autumn blew around.

Now the message was complete. All eleven numbers had a letter next to it. When they read it horizontally, it read *Creaky Stair*.

THE CREAKY STAIR

Sam knew exactly what step the letter was talking about, and Grace knew, too. Obviously, the "creak" was something that nobody missed.

Hurrying down the halls, they made their way toward the stairwell that led up to the lighthouse Watch. Both of their hearts were racing so fast they could hardly contain the excitement. These clues were real, and they were left so that they would be found. Who knew how long it had been since Charlotte had left all of this? Neither Sam nor Grace had any idea, but it seemed as if it was all left just for them.

In the stairwell, they hurried up the steps until they came to the stair the creaked louder than the rest. But the question was, where was the clue? Every step was made of wood, so Grace looked for any little form of writing. She looked for a word of some sort or maybe a scrap of paper hidden in the corners.

Sam let her search for a little while, but he was thinking about how creaky the stair was. If a step is creaky, it means the board is loose.

Grace finally stopped because she hadn't found anything. "Maybe the letters have to be put in a different order..."

Sam pulled up on the board, and it came off like nobody's business.

"Or we could just do that..." Grace finished.

Below, there was a space the size of the whole stair step. Grace reached in and felt around. There was a wrinkled envelope at the bottom of the nook. She pulled it out, blowing the dust off of it. Sam replaced the board, and they went back to the kitchen to read the note.

Grace ripped open the envelope and dumped out the contents. There was a key, and a scrap of paper, which read:

Dear Prejudiced Pin,

Think only of the past as its remembrance gives you pleasure...
J. A.

"That's all it says," Grace said.

"That makes no sense. No sense at all."

"I don't get why it says "Dear Prejudiced Pin," but the line below it might be a quote of some sort," Grace suggested.

"And who is J. A.?"

"Well," Grace said. "If it's a quote, then the J.A. would probably be the person who said the quote..."

"Dear prejudiced pin?"

"I think the first line is a code of some sort..." Grace went on.

"Like what?"

"Like maybe the letters were scrambled into words?"

Sam pulled out a pencil and paper and began writing different combinations of the letters.

Grace looked over the line in the middle. The words seemed to ring a bell, though she couldn't quite place them. She thought it was interesting for Charlotte to write this on a note, as it was something that Grace needed to hear. She should think of her past, but only the happy parts of it. She had been too pained to think of her parents because it reminded her that they were gone.

In reality, she should be thinking of all of the wonderful moments she had spent with them. She had over a decade of memories that filled her life's treasure box, and it was as if she had dumped it all into the ocean because it was too painful to think about.

This strange little quote said something far more than it seemed like it should have, and Grace knew she needed to hear it, and somehow, it seemed like her aunt needed it, too.

But then, Grace looked at the J.A. The first name to pop into her head was her favorite author – Jane Austen. And then everything clicked.

"It's Pride and Prejudice," Grace said suddenly.

"What?"

"Try making those words into the title Pride and Prejudice . "J.A." stands for Jane Austen, and that quote is from the book. Elizabeth shares her philosophy with Mr. Darcy. He disagrees with her, explaining that painful recollections intrude... and they should be repelled, and then he goes on and explains that he was a selfish being. He says that she taught him a lesson, but she never expected him to turn around like this... She never thought things would change. What Elizabeth meant to say was that she had forgiven him... for what he had done when he completely ridiculed her on his first impressions..."

Grace had read the book so many times, and she was choking up now. She hadn't expected Charlotte's message to come with so much force. She was telling Grace to forgive. She was saying to always look for the good, even though the bad is too much to see through at times – there is still good.

Sam didn't understand, again, except he knew that Pride and Prejudice was a book, and he knew there was a copy in his uncle's library.

"I know where the book is."

Grace wiped away the tears and laughed a little. "Remember the good things in the past..."

...

In the library, finding Pride and Prejudice turned out to be more like finding a needle in the haystack. There was no call number or sorting system, so they had to just look. Grace took a bookshelf, and Sam took another. Grace had no idea what size the book was, either. She knew there were paperback editions, hardcover editions, and many more.

The book was originally published in the early 1800's – like two centuries ago, and there had been countless editions of it printed since. Grace had her own copy of the book, though hers was a very modern printing.

Sam, on the other hand, must have seen the book in the library before, so he at least had an idea. After several minutes of silent searching, Sam found the book.

"Try shaking it to check if there are any loose pieces of paper in it."

Sam did as Grace directed. He tried for a while, but with no success.

"Do you think there might be letters inside of the book? Maybe there's a letter on a page or something."

Sam flipped through the book, but still there was not a sign of anything.

"Let me see it." Grace took the book.

It was an older printing of the book. The cover was worn and faded, though the stamped-gold lettering still shimmered. There was a gold border that went around the outside on the front and the back. The rest of the book was a deep green.

On the cover, there was a rectangle in the top corner that read: Jane Austen – Pride and Prejudice. Grace instinctively opened the book and smelled it. She loved the smell of old books. The paper had a different scent than the newer books did. The pages were slightly yellowed, and the text seemed unusual, but it was still the book.

Grace wondered if she had been wrong about the message, but she couldn't see what else the message might have meant. The title had unscrambled to Pride and Prejudice , and she was sure the quote came from the book. It was too obvious. The "J.A." stood for Jane Austen – it had to. She couldn't see how they could be wrong in believing the message led them to the book, but then again, there wasn't another clue in sight.

Just then, Grace felt curious about when the book had been published, so she flipped to the front of the book to see the publication date.

There, in the corner of the book, was a message:

I hope you enjoy this book as much as I have...
– Lottie

"Look, Sam, this is the right book." Grace pointed to the note.

Sam took the book and read the note. "That can't be the next clue, though. Can it?"

"It doesn't seem like it is..." Grace agreed.

She took the book back and began looking it over again.

"I sure hope she doesn't want us to read it..." Sam groaned. He had never been much of a reader.

"I've read it."

"You have?"

"Of course – it's a wonderful book. That's how I knew the quote from the last clue."

"Yeah, right..." Sam said. "I don't really want to read it."

"You ought to."

"But it's a girly book isn't it?"

"Some people might think of it that way, but I think it's one that anyone can get something out of. Anyway, I don't think that she meant for us to read it to find the clue," Grace reassured. "I think it was a gift... to her friend."

"The other person in the locket?"

"Right."

As Grace said the word, she noticed a small seam along the crease of the cover. As she looked closer, she realized that the place behind the binding had been cut. And there, between the binding and the block of the book, there was a tiny, folded up piece of paper.

With her fingernails, Grace carefully drew out the paper. It was somewhat difficult, but it was manageable.

"I found it, Sam," she breathed.

She held out the piece of paper for Sam to see.

"Where was that?" he asked.

Grace showed Sam the seam in the book and the little crack it formed. Sam gloated over it for a moment. He went on and on about how amazing and clever it had been to hide the clue in the crack. "I probably never would have found it," Sam concluded.

"That's because you need to be more thorough of a searcher."

"What do you mean? I'm thorough. I mean, I've found a lot of the clues," Sam argued.

"But sometimes you have to trust a little more than just your senses."

"What's that supposed to mean?" Sam frowned.

"Sometimes you have to follow your gut feelings..."

THE JEWELRY BOX

In the kitchen, all of the clues they had found during the day were strewn across the table. There was the key and the envelope, the message from the lantern and the painting, but none of those clues were important right now, though each one was important at the time that it had been opened. They had the newest clue, and it claimed all of their attention.

Here in the kitchen, Grace noticed the weather outside. It was still raining, but it was also getting late in the day. "Sam, I better go. I mean, I don't want it to get too late..."

"But couldn't we just do one more clue?" Sam begged.

"We don't know how long it will take us, and I know that once we open it, there's no way we're going to stop after that. I'd better just go – before the next clue. I'll come back tomorrow, though. You can count on that," Grace was already picking up her umbrella and coat.

...

Soon Grace was gone, and the lighthouse was silent again. Sam suddenly felt alone, again remembering that his uncle was gone. The book <u>Pride and Prejudice</u> sat on the table with the clue sitting on top of it.

For a moment, Sam felt the urge to open the note and see what it read. It was almost too hard for him to hold back, but he decided that he could be patient until Grace returned the next day.

Sam did, though, pick up the book again. Grace had said that <u>Pride and Prejudice</u> was a good book. Charlotte had also recommended it, and Sam had nothing better to do. It was a cold, rainy day, and a book actually sort of sounded like a nice thing, so Sam took the book from the table to his room and tossed it onto his bed. Then he went to the window and cranked it open. The sound of the rain, the ocean, the wind, and the thunder performed a beautiful concerto of wonderful sounds.

It wasn't storming very hard outside. Even the thunder was just rumbles every now and again, and soon the room had cooled down, filling with the scent of the rain and the ocean breeze.

Sam lay on his bed and opened the book. The room was a little too cool now, so he pulled out his blanket – an old, brown blanket. It was kind of scratchy, but he still liked it nonetheless.

And then, when everything in the moment was perfect, he started to read.

...

Grace enjoyed her walk home. Because the day was lighter now, she could see everything a lot better. The gray sky and falling rain was beautiful in her eyes. She personally preferred sunny days, but this rain was still peaceful. She watched the breeze among the branches, as it lifted them up and back again.

Though she didn't quite know what would happen if she ran into her aunt, Grace didn't want to climb the trellis for fear that she might slip on it while it was wet, and she also didn't know how she would get the umbrella back downstairs if she took it up that way.

She was left no other choice, but to enter the house through the front door. Realizing now, that the house was awfully close, she began figuring out different possible scenarios.

When she reached the house, she climbed up the steps to the front door. Holding the umbrella out in front of her, she shook the rain off of it. Then she closed it and opened the door.

Right away she could smell bread baking in the oven. The light was on in the kitchen, and without even turning around she knew that she had to face her aunt.

"Oh hello, Grace," she said. "I was just starting dinner. What have you been up to? It's bitter weather out there today. Don't you think so?"

"I took a walk," Grace said simply. It was true that she had taken a walk, but it wasn't completely everything she had done.

"This I see."

"I love walking in the rain. I mean, sometimes at least. It's not too stormy out there, so I thought it would be a good thing. It enlivens your senses," Grace found herself rambling.

"And it can give you a horrific cough. You can catch a cold going out in weather like that," her aunt warned.

Grace shrugged. "Sometimes it's worth it."

Her aunt laughed. "You remind me of myself – how crazy I used to be." She sighed.

"Well... I'd better go change," Grace said after a pause.

"Right," her aunt agreed.

Then Grace was free. She had rushed from the room so quickly, that she had taken the folded up umbrella with her.

"Oh dear," Grace thought.

Now she would have to figure out how to get it back downstairs without a scene, but that could wait for later. For now, she just stood it up against the wall in her closet.

Next, Grace went straight to the window and opened it. The breeze was cool and gentle, and she breathed it in for a moment. The day had been an exciting one for Grace, and her mind was still racing over everything that had happened.

Finding the picture in the basement and following the clues that Charlotte had left had almost made Grace feel like she knew her. It seemed as if Charlotte had left the messages just for Grace, though she still had yet to figure out why.

For a moment, she sat on her bed and drew out the locket from where it was concealed under her shirt. She opened it and looked at the pictures for a moment. Charlotte seemed to be someone who Grace would have gotten along with really well. While, on the other hand, the guy in the other picture seemed like a complete stranger. Grace wished she knew more about him, and she guessed that when she did, she would find a lot more of the answers she was searching for.

She knew Charlotte. She knew her like a friend.

Grace decided that her journal deserved to be in on some of the secrets, so she pulled it out from where it was hiding underneath her pillow and wrote. There was a lot to write, so the words just came. They seemed to come like the falling rain and collect like puddles on her page.

...

Sam looked up when it was nearly dark. He had read several chapters of the book. Not understanding completely what Grace thought was so endearing about it, he marked the page and left the book on his bed.

He thought of his uncle. It had been a full two days since he had left, and Sam was beginning to get worried. It wasn't like his uncle to leave for this long. But again, the message told Sam not to worry, so he tried his best to ignore the nagging thoughts.

When Grace had been there, they didn't stop for lunch, so Sam was getting hungry. He went to the kitchen and made himself a cup of warm soup. Looking at the kitchen table covered with the clues they had found, Sam wondered what his uncle would say if he saw the mess.

Sam just shrugged and went up to his room. He still didn't have anything better to do, so he returned to the book. Something made him want to read it, even though he didn't really like it. The words were a little too flowery for him, but he still continued to read – thinking of Grace and hoping it would get better.

...

The next morning it was raining again. Grace didn't want to have to go back down to the kitchen. Her aunt seemed to be getting a little suspicious of her, so Grace decided to take the umbrella and risk going down the trellis.

Her heart was beating in her throat as she carefully climbed over the side of the balcony. She had the tie of the umbrella around her wrist as she climbed down, and she was more than happy when she could finally feel the soggy ground beneath her feet when she jumped to the ground.

The whole lawn was filled with soggy grass, and in some places there were collecting puddles. It was raining harder as well, and Grace was drenched before she could even open the umbrella.

She was so anxious to get to Sam and figure out the next clues that she took off running down her aunt's drive.

What Grace didn't know was that her aunt was peeking through the kitchen window as she made her escape. At first she had just dismissed it as Grace's usual, strange self, but then she began wondering, seeing how Grace had climbed down the trellis instead of coming through the kitchen. It was all beginning to seem too suspicious.

...

When Sam had awoken, he found his face in the book he had been reading the night before, and the first thing that came to his mind was Grace and the mystery that they were working to solve. It seemed like they had to be getting close to the end – whatever it was.

Though Sam hadn't really thought of it before, he wondered what this was all leading to. He wondered why Charlotte had left messages, and he also wondered why she had everything hidden in the lighthouse.

It was a good thing that Sam woke up when he did because Grace had already reached the lighthouse by then. She knocked on the door and waited for an answer. It took a while before he made it to the door, and she tapped her foot impatiently.

In the kitchen, breakfast didn't matter. They pounced on the message they had found in the book and opened it:

Diamonds of the sea,
Adorning a box,
In simple beauty it waits –
Its treasure to be claimed.

"Diamonds of the sea?" Grace asked.
"Pearls maybe?"

"That doesn't make sense though. Is there a box adorned by pearls?" Grace wondered.

"Not that I know of."

"Then it doesn't make sense," Grace said.

"Diamonds of the sea. Adorning a box..." Sam thought aloud. "I really don't get it."

"Wait! It's talking about seashells, and there's a box on the mantel in the sitting room – a jewelry box or something. It is locked, but..." Grace rummaged through the pile of clues for the envelope that they had found in the stairwell. Then she pulled out the key and showed it to Sam. "That must be why we have this."

THE GLOBE

They hurried to the sitting room and straight for the mantel. Then they carefully lifted the box down to the floor so that they could see it better. Grace, who was still holding the key, inserted it carefully into the lock.

"What if the key doesn't work?" Sam asked suddenly.

"Then I was wrong, and we'll have to figure out what the clue is really talking about..."

Sam nodded.

But the key did work. It slipped right into the keyhole, and it clicked when Grace turned it. Ever so cautiously, they lifted the lid to the box. It seemed like the box was extra fragile because it was made completely out of shells, so they were very cautious.

Inside, there was a box made of glass. The shells had actually been either glued or attached in some way to the glass box, which had the hinges and the keyhole. Inside the box, were several items: there was a gold coin, several necklaces, pearls, seashells... it almost seemed to them as if they had found a long-lost treasure.

But at the same time, it seemed like they had just opened something that had always been found. To Sam, this wasn't a discovery at all. He had seen the box many times and had never really cared what was in it. He thought it was neat to finally see inside, but he hoped there was more to Charlotte's mystery than this.

"Is this it?" he asked. "I mean is this all we were looking for?"

Grace shrugged. She felt disappointed, too. This didn't help them figure out who the boy in the locket was, and it didn't even tell them very much more about Charlotte. Was it really all a treasure hunt to find her jewelry box?

Then Grace tipped the box over, gently dumping out all of its contents. Just as she hoped, at the very bottom of the box, folded so perfectly that it clung to the bottom, was an envelope. It had been pushed inside so carefully that anyone who was just looking for treasure would have stopped before finding it.

Grace and Sam were looking more and more, though they still didn't really know what for, just that they were looking. Grace still had questions that needed to be answered.

Sam reached in and carefully pulled out the envelope. He tore it open and pulled out the paper inside:

> *Round and round,*
> *I keep spinning round,*
> *Turning day to night,*
> *Taking light from sight...*

"Okay," Grace said. "This one is really weird."

"No kidding. What spins and takes light away?" Sam started to laugh.

"Is it something that has light in it? Maybe something that has to do with the lighthouse?"

"Well, there's the light in the lighthouse, but it doesn't turn around," Sam explained.

"But how do you turn it on? Isn't there something that you turn? Like a crank or something?"

Sam was trying really hard, but the idea wasn't clicking. He shook his head. To turn the lighthouse on was more like flipping on a switch. It had a fuse that was lit – like a candle, but he couldn't think of how it took light from sight.

"Do you think they light the lighthouse differently than they used to? Is there, like a crank or something that would move the wick up and down?" Grace was still focused on the clue.

It still wasn't making sense. "Not that I know of. My uncle said they would just light it, instead of flipping a switch, and I don't really see what the lighthouse has to do with turning day to night."

"You're right," Grace said.

She stopped for a moment, thinking hard. When she thought about day turning to night, she thought about the earth. The earth would spin, and it was what would change day to night. It didn't matter where you were on the earth. When your side of the earth was facing the sun, it was daytime, and when that side moved around and was facing away from the sun, it was night. It was a simple fact.

What wasn't simple was how and why this clue would be talking about the earth. For sure the clue was on the earth, somewhere. Grace was even pretty sure that the clue was in the lighthouse itself. All of the other clues had been... she started thinking out loud, "I think the clue is talking about the earth, and how it rotates – changing night to day."

Sam nodded in agreement. After a moment of thinking, Sam had it. "I know where it is!"

"Where?"

"It's got to be somewhere with the globe in library. It's a model of the earth that spins and changes night to day."

...

In the library, they searched all around the globe. The first thing they did was tip the globe upside-down, to see if there was a message taped to the bottom of it, but there wasn't anything there, so they searched the globe. They looked for little letters on it – none. They looked for something on the ring that held the globe. Again, they couldn't find anything.

Then they started looking on the stand that the globe stood on. Still, there wasn't a trace of any clue.

"Maybe it isn't the globe," Sam said at last.

Grace wanted it to be the globe – it was the only thing that had made sense. While she thought, her hands instinctively spun the globe. She had always loved playing with globes. She would play the "vacation game" where she would spin the globe and close her eyes. Then she would stop the globe with her finger, and wherever her finger landed was where she said she wanted to go. Sometimes, in fact almost a third of the time, she'd land out in the middle of the ocean.

All of these thoughts raced through her mind as she spun the globe, watching as the landmasses went round and round.

"What's that sound?" Sam said suddenly.

"What sound?" Grace snapped out of her trance.

"That funny, scraping sound when you turn the globe."

Grace couldn't hear anything but the whirring of the globe on its stand.

"It sounds like there's something inside of it," Sam went on.

Grace's heart was racing now, hoping, hoping there was something inside.

Sam picked up the globe and shook it. Sure enough, there was a rattling sound as something moved up and down inside.

"How in the world would it get in there?" Grace asked.

Sam showed her how the globe had a seam that ran around the middle – where the equator was. "It splits into two halves here," he said.

There was a hole in the top, and a hole in the bottom. These two holes were what the globe spun on. The stand had two fingers that stuck out, one in each hole. This was what held the globe in place.

Sam lifted the globe and got the globe off of the finger on the bottom. Then he lowered the globe to release it completely from the stand. Next, he carefully took the two halves of the globe apart.

The inside of the globe was brown with funny shaped supports that made the shape of the globe. It was strange looking at it from this view, but there, in the bottom of the bottom half, was a little, folded-up scrap of paper – the next clue.

"That's it," Grace breathed.

Just then, a lightning bolt sent a shiver through the whole lighthouse, and the thunder came immediately after. It was so loud they could both feel the rumble in the ground beneath them. This turned their attention from the clue they had found to the weather outside.

The storm was picking up fast. What had been a gentle rain was now a pouring torrent. Rain was falling so thick that it was hard to see even a few feet ahead. The rain fell like a blanket that hid everything from view.

...

Grace's aunt had seen the lightning, too, and she had also noticed the rain. In her mind, thoughts were spinning fast. She was worried about Grace. The storm was so powerful now; it was dangerous for anyone to be out in the rain. Grace still hadn't come home, so matters were beginning to get concerning.

THE TELESCOPE

Once the globe was back in one piece and sitting back on its stand, Grace opened the note:

To see what you cannot see,
You have to look with more than your eyes.
To find what you cannot find,
You have to search with more than your mind.
Look for distant shores,
And you'll find me...

"Okay..." Sam said. "Where do we start?"

To Grace the riddle was about looking. This seemed like something that Sam would understand better than herself. He was always looking for things. The riddle talked about looking with more than just your eyes and searching with more than your mind, but that didn't make sense.

"Are the last two lines clues?" Grace asked. "Look for distant shores, and you'll find me..."

Both Sam and Grace knew that the clue had to be talking about something material, though it seemed to be talking about searching, and how you should search – almost a "do good" quote. But just knowing how to look didn't help them find the next clue. It didn't help anything.

"Well, if we're supposed to be looking for distant shores, we'd better go to the window," Sam suggested.

It sounded practical to Grace, though it seemed like the riddle would have explained more about which window. What were the distant shores it was talking about?

They first went to the window in the kitchen and looked out into the rain. It was a spectacular storm. Sam started checking the window seal.

"Sometimes the board at the bottom of the window can be pried off. I've seen that sort of hiding place before." He tried to wiggle the board, but it had been hammered in firmly.

From the kitchen, they moved through the lighthouse, checking window after window. They went through the library and the sitting room, and soon they had checked all of the windows but without any success.

It was a long, belaboring search, and the worst part of it was that in the end, there was nothing to show. None of the boards on the window seals were loose. There hadn't been anything hidden in the curtains or in the cracks – nothing.

Grace thought about the note again. Yes, you had to look out of the window to see distant shores, but that wasn't what the whole message said. The clue spoke of looking with more than just your eyes. A window was just a window. It wasn't more than your eyes – it was just your eyes.

"We're supposed to look through something..." Grace said. "That's what the clue says first."

"But what? The window is something you can look through."

"Something that makes it so that you can see more than just what your eyes see," Grace continued.

"You mean like binoculars or something?"

Now they were getting closer, Grace could tell. She knew that everything that the clues had talked about was material, and binoculars were something tangible that you could see, feel, and take apart for that matter.

Sam went to get his binoculars from his room, and when Grace saw them, she knew that they weren't what the clue was talking about. They were too shiny and new to be something Charlotte could have hid something in.

"Isn't there something like binoculars that's older around the lighthouse?"

It took just a second, but they both thought of it at exactly the same time – the telescope!

Telescopes were used to see distant shores, and they were more than just your eyes. They could help you see things beyond what you could see by yourself, and best of all, there was an old telescope in the library.

Within moments they were looking at the telescope with new eyes. Sam had first thought that you used the telescope to see the next clue, but Grace assured him that the telescope had to be taken apart in order to find the message.

For just a moment, they looked at the thing, not daring to disassemble it. The thing was a treasure trove of hiding places. There were a million nooks and tons of niches. Sam had never looked at the telescope like this before. He could tell that Charlotte was a genius in figuring out hiding places. Just realizing that these clues had been hidden for who knew how long and completely beneath his nose made Sam feel all the more amazed by Charlotte's hiding-clue skills.

"Where in the world do you think the clue is hiding?" Sam asked.

"It could be anywhere."

"And what if we take it all apart, but then we can't remember how it went back together?" he worried.

"Well, that would be bad," Grace said.

It was true. The telescope had so many eyepieces and lenses that it would be almost like looking for a needle in a haystack if they tried to find a clue inside the telescope, and Grace also knew that Sam's fear was a sensible one. Finally, Sam insisted they check the outside of the telescope before they unscrewed anything.

Sam looked all around the stand. They even moved the telescope out of its place to see if something was hiding underneath it, but all of this came to no avail.

"All right," Sam said at last. "We can take it apart – but only one piece at a time. Where do we start?"

Grace had been figuring out a practical way to take the telescope apart by thinking of the clue.

"Well, the clue says 'Look for distant shores and you'll find me...' so I think something must be hidden in the area that you look through."

They started by removing the eyepiece. It would have been a great place to hide a clue, but there was nothing in there.

The next easiest thing to remove was the scope – the longest part of the telescope. It unscrewed from the front of the telescope, and inside was a clue larger than both Sam and Grace had anticipated.

It took up the whole scope to fit it, wrapped around the outside. Anybody who looked through the telescope would have never guessed it was there, but there it was, and there it had been for a long, long time.

Grace turned the scope upside-down and shook it gently until the roll of paper slid out, onto the table. Before they opened it, they reassembled the telescope, and then Sam had to look through it really quick – just to be sure everything still worked right.

Grace unrolled the roll of paper on the table.

It was a map of the lighthouse. There were several different pages with different layers showing the different stories of the lighthouse. The tower was on a page all its own – all of the stairs were sketched out and shaded accordingly.

To Sam, looking at those blueprints, he felt as if he had found the inner-workings of the lighthouse, and they were truly a wonder. All of the pipe work was drawn out. He could see where closets and rooms aligned. It was suddenly like he could see through the walls in the house. He had a big picture.

But while he was exulting over the blue prints and just seeing them, Grace was avidly scanning each page. She had discovered quickly that there wasn't any text message on any of the blue prints. She thought this was strange, but she kept searching – knowing that there was a clue hidden somewhere on the pages.

After a couple moments, she noticed several dots around the house. A hairline connected them all together. Grace looked at the dots carefully. They seemed to be somewhat random, and there were several in the library, one in the sitting room... and then Grace realized what they were. The dots showed where Charlotte had hidden all of her clues around the lighthouse.

Grace followed the line as it wound through the various rooms in the lighthouse. It went up into the lighthouse tower with a dot on the step that creaked – where they had found the key. But the line didn't stop there. It kept on going. As Grace leaned in for a closer look, she realized that there were tiny letters on the steps. Starting at the lowest step, she put the message together:

Climb the stairs to the top,
Climb the stairs to the stars.
Light awaits you in the end.
My secret's waiting round the bend...

"Sam," Grace said, "We have to go up into the light tower."

"What? Why?"

Grace didn't answer. She picked up the blueprint of the tower and rushed from the room. Sam had the choice to be left or to follow. Of course he hurried after her.

As they climbed the stairs, Grace explained. "There's a message written on the stair steps." She read it to Sam.

At the top of the stairwell, she threw the door open, entering the main gallery. It was pouring rain, and within moments, she and Sam were completely drenched. They climbed into the Watch and pulled the glass door shut behind them.

Grace studied the page in her hands for a moment. The hairline path she had been following stopped here.

"What now?" Sam asked.

"I don't know..." Grace said. "It just leads us here..."

THE SECRET OF THE LIGHTHOUSE

Grace looked around the Watch for a moment. Everything inside was silent, but outside the winds were howling and the rains pouring. Grace looked carefully across the room. The floor was made up of tiles. She began pushing at them with her feet.

Sam did the same. All of them were tightened down – except for one.

It didn't wiggle very much when Sam pushed on it, but it shifted just a hair. "Look at this," he said.

Grace hurried next to him and tried the tile with her own foot. She wasn't sure if it was loose enough to pull out, but they both got down on their knees and tried to pull it out. It was hard to get their fingers underneath it, but once they did, the tile lifted.

The reason why it hadn't been very loose was because half of it was on hinges. It was a compartment in the floor.

It was dusty inside and kind of deep. It was deep enough that everything inside vanished into darkness. Sam reached in, and at arm's length he reached the bottom of it. He felt around for a moment.

He shook his head. "Nope. Nothing's in there."

Grace sighed. Maybe someone else had found it already, or maybe this was the wrong place...

"Wait," Sam said. "I feel something in here."

His fingers had touched something rectangular. Closing his hand around it, he brought it up into the light. It was a parcel wrapped in a paper sack.

"What is it?" Grace breathed.

"There's only one way to find out."

They both ripped the paper off – too excited to be careful any longer.

Inside, there was a book. It had a dark blue cover with a stenciled lighthouse on the front. The corners of the cover were sewn and rounded. The pages inside were slightly yellowed with age, but other than that, it was in pristine shape.

"A book?" Sam said.

Grace took it and opened it. Page after page was filled with the same handwriting that had been on all of the clues – a perfectly slanted cursive. She flipped all of the way through to the end. It was filled, every page, with words.

"It's a diary!" Grace said.

Sam's face showed disappointment. "And what's so great about that?"

"Don't you get it? It's the Charlotte's journal! This is her story in her own words. She hid her journal... for someone to find in the future."

"Us?"

"Yes."

To Grace, this was the greatest treasure she could have found. Somehow she felt as if she needed to understand Charlotte, like she needed to know her story because it seemed like Charlotte's story had a lot to do with Grace's. It was almost like the two tales were intermingled somehow. Only Charlotte's was finished and written in ink, but Grace's continued where the other had ended.

Grace knew that she needed this book, and holding it in her hands, she almost felt as if she had been given a time machine that would transport her directly to Charlotte's time.

Tears were gathering in Grace's eyes. In the blur of her vision, she could almost see Charlotte bending over the hole in the ground. She imagined Charlotte kissing the book in a final farewell and setting it carefully inside. Grace had never felt like this. She had never felt like someone was this close to her, almost as if the ghost of Charlotte was in the room, haunting her now.

Grace flipped the book open to the inside cover. In neat lettering was Charlotte's whole name, but Grace went white as she read it. "No... way..." she whispered.

"What? What is it, Grace?"

She couldn't even speak. She was so surprised. Her throat was suddenly dry, and her heart was beating ever so quickly.

"What?" Sam asked again. "You look as if you've seen a ghost!"

Grace still hadn't recovered from her shock, so Sam took the book from her and looked at the inside cover – Charlotte Happs.

It was the last name that had astounded Grace. Charlotte had the same last name as Grace, and that meant that Grace was somehow related. That meant that Charlotte wasn't just a mystery that Grace had happened upon, but that they were connected genetically. Now Grace suddenly understood why she felt so close to Charlotte. The tears were falling now.

Questions were beginning to swell up in her mind so quickly. They were coming all over again.

Grace shook her head. "I can't believe it. I knew she looked familiar..." Grace pulled out the locket and opened it. "But I had never realized that she looked familiar because she was related to me."

Sam took another look at the girl in the locket. Grace had some distinguishable differences, but now that he was looking for similarities, he could see them. She had the same brown hair, and her mouth rested in the same form. Her nose was a little different, but of all the features, their eyes were the same. They were deep and brown, and staring into those eyes, Sam knew he could easily get lost.

Suddenly there were lights from outside the lighthouse. It was raining so hard neither Sam nor Grace could see the car through the rain-streaked windows, but the fact that they were car lights was undeniable.

"Is that my uncle?" Sam said. "Is he back? Finally?"

DARKNESS

Sam bolted from the Watch, leaving the door open behind him. Grace stuffed the journal underneath her shirt to keep it safe from the rain. She hurried to follow until she saw the car, recognizing it in an instant – it was her aunt's car.

Through the rain, she could see her aunt shielding her eyes to see. Grace had been caught.

"Grace Happs, get down here this instant!" she yelled.

Grace sluggishly came down the stairs. She knew this was the end of everything. On the stairs she called to Sam. "I'm really sorry about this. It's my aunt out there."

"Your aunt? How did she know you were here?"

"I don't know," Grace admitted. She was trembling now, half from fear and half from crying. "She's never going to let me see you again..."

"And you're going to let her do that?" Sam was defiant.

"What else can I do?"

"You can't just give in. I mean, there's got to be some way."

"Sam, I can't think of a way. I just can't. It's impossible. This is it – it's over."

"No. I won't let it. Grace, you're my only friend... you mean a lot to me."

Grace was crying again with a new emotion. "And you're everything to me, too..." She hugged Sam. "I guess this is goodbye?"

"If I could change things I would. I really would." She could see Sam choking up a little; his bottom lip trembled as he spoke. Though he tried to be strong and macho, he couldn't keep everything back. He knew this was a real goodbye.

"I would change things, too. And who knows? Things just might change."

Sam suddenly grabbed Grace's hand. He pressed something cold and smooth into her palm and closed her hand around it. "I want you to have this..." he said.

Grace didn't even have to look at it – she knew exactly what it was. "Your pocket watch?"

Sam nodded.

"I'm sorry, Sam. I'm really sorry. I didn't mean to break you like this. You probably would've been better off if you never ran into me. I'm so sorry."

"You're not sorry," Sam spoke desperately. "Don't ever be sorry about what happened. It was meant to be. Really, it was. Always think of this summer with fond remembrance."

"No, I can't. It'll always bring back tears. You were the light that pushed away the clouds. You helped me forget what I came from... and now, I don't want to let you go."

"There's nothing left for us to do... You have to go."
Then Grace stiffened. "No, I won't." She stood
there, firm on the stair. "I won't go."

Suddenly the door to the stairwell opened and her
aunt stood there in the doorway. "Grace, I trusted
you! And you deliberately disobeyed me." Her aunt
was climbing the stairs.

"I won't go..." Grace whispered to Sam.

"The lighthouse will always be burning for you.
Don't ever let your light go out. Never..." Their eyes
connected for a moment.

Grace's aunt had grabbed her arm now. "Child, I
was not fooling around when I told you I would send
you back to the orphanage because I will. And really,
you deserve just that – right now! If you don't obey
my rules, you can't live under my roof!"

Grace turned on her. "Your rules are unjust... you
just don't understand, do you? You don't. You can't,"
Grace was sobbing. "You could never understand.
You don't know what it means to really care about
someone."

At this, Clarenne half dragged and shoved Grace
from the lighthouse into the pouring rain. She
opened the car door and pushed her inside. Grace
covered her face as she fell sobbing onto the passenger seat.

Clarenne climbed into the other side of the car and
took off down the road.

Grace looked out her rear-view mirror at the lighthouse. She knew this was the last time she would
see it. The door was thrown open, and Sam stood
there silhouetted by the light within. Grace cried as

she watched him getting smaller and smaller into the distance.

Soon the car turned the bend, and he was gone from sight.

Grace cried again, covering her face with one hand and clutching at the book under her shirt with the other. The life that she had found, free from her old past, had come crashing down like a tidal wave upon her, and it just added to the pain she had felt before. The wound of her parents' passing felt as if it had been sliced open again with a bitter blade. Every time a wound reopens, it has a harder time healing, and though it eventually heals, there is always a scar that remains. Always.

...

Sam stood in the doorway of the lighthouse until the car was gone. Now his tears erupted like a hurricane. He couldn't just stand there. Sam bolted from the doorway, running faster than he had ever run before. He bolted across the beach, picking up speed as he went. The puddles from the storms that had held for the past days sloshed all over him as he ran through.

He was drenched by rain, sand, and tears, but he didn't care. He didn't care about anything. Nothing mattered to him anymore because the one thing that he had was now taken away. The wind blew in his face, and his eyes stung with tears. He couldn't see where he was going, and he didn't care.

He ran like the wind – everything rushing past. He let his tears blow behind him with the rain. He ran. He felt the wind whip his fears away.

At last Sam's legs started to cramp, but it didn't matter. His stomach was on fire, and his breathing was forced. He had run farther than he had ever run before in a single stretch. He could feel himself growing faint. All of his physical begged him to stop, but his emotion overruled it.

He ran on, pushing himself past all limits. When his breath began to fail him, he slowed. The tide hit his bare feet, coming up around his ankles, pulling the sand as it rushed away. He ran into the tide, not caring if it carried him away. Emotions were swelling so high within him; he was drowning in emotions.

The ocean was in a fury from the storm. A tidal wave was building in front of him. As Sam ran farther into the water, it rose to his chest. He let go of his footing and began swimming with a fury – straight for the tidal wave. Choking on tears and water, he swam on into the current.

When it reached him, it buried him. He couldn't tell which way was up or which was down. Now he began to fight. He tried to tread water, trying to find a breath, but the waves crashing over his head buried him and held him down. In his mind, he could see Grace's face. He knew that if he could see her again, everything would be all right, that she could bring him back to the surface and turn the darkness into light.

But Grace was gone, and Sam knew that. She wouldn't be able to help him, so he struggled on alone. His air was running out; he began choking for a breath, but there was none. He asked himself why he had brought himself out in the ocean. It wasn't to drown, but he was so many feet beneath the water, not knowing which way was up. Trying to survive became his purpose.

But even as his purpose, it wasn't enough. Sam couldn't fight the torrent that pulled him down. Looking out through the water, he could see an endless expanse of grays. It was all a blur, a ripple of light and dark. He had never felt so lost and so alone as he did now in the ocean.

It was so infinite, and he was so small, so lost and confused.

Sam's lack of breath was pulling him into unconscious, and soon his struggling stopped. His eyes slowly closed, and everything faded into darkness.

...

The ship was rocking back and forth in the current. Sam's uncle held on tight, and his heart was racing. This was a déjà vu experience for him, and he was afraid. A wave crashed over the small, fishing boat, nearly tipping it over. The small motor on the back wasn't enough to keep it from going where the wave threw it.

Another wave rose ten feet above the boat, and this one capsized the boat. Splinters and driftwood scattered away from him. The wave had pushed Sam's uncle so deep beneath the water that he had to struggle to get right side up again.

Finally, with his head above, he gasped for a breath. Then he paddled over to the nearest piece of driftwood, holding on for dear life. He looked around for help. There was no land in sight, and there was no sign that the storm was letting up. He had but one choice – to hold on to the broken floorboards and hope that he would come out on top of every wave that crashed over his head.

As the waves whipped him to and fro, Sam's uncle looked off into the distance. He thought he could see someone walking on the water, someone he recognized from a long time ago.

"Is it... is it really you?" he called.

But the figure didn't hear him. She just walked on.

"Come back... come back," he wailed.

But she was gone.

THE STORM

Grace didn't say a word when the car reached the white house. She just bolted from the car, up the stairs and the ladder, all of the way to her room. Her tears were falling like nothing she could hold back or stop now.

She slammed the door behind her and locked it. Then she fell, face first, onto her bed. She sobbed for hours.

All of the crying made her weak, and after a long while, she had cried herself into a restless sleep.

...

When she finally awoke, it was even darker than before – well into the evening, but she wasn't tired anymore.

She started evaluating her feelings. First of all, she had let everyone down. She didn't feel like Sam was the only one she had let down. She felt like she had somehow let her parents down, and of course she had let her aunt down. She even felt that she had let Charlotte down.

There was so much emptiness inside, and Grace couldn't find a place to turn for help. It was as if she was out in the storm, and she needed a place to hide and find shelter, but all she could do was fall apart. She wanted comfort; she needed comfort from somewhere.

She wanted to rush to her drawer and get out the picture of her mom and dad and just hug it close, but she knew they were gone, and they wouldn't be coming back. She couldn't hold on to them any-more. She thought about Sam. She wanted to hold on to the pocket watch – but Sam was gone, too. She thought of her aunt – she was hollow and full of a hate so strong that she couldn't forgive, and she would never really be able to love anyone. She wouldn't make Grace feel safe.

To Grace, it seemed that there was no use in loving at all. It just made her fall to pieces. The only thing Grace knew to do was to let her heart glaze over with the ice of not caring. The bitter cold would numb the pain, taking away all emotions. It would keep her from loving, or caring, or feeling. It was the only thing left.

But Grace didn't want a cold heart. She realized that was what her aunt had done. Feeling pain would be better than feeling nothing at all.

Then Charlotte's diary came to her mind. Grace re-alized she could hold on to the past that Charlotte had left. The past that was scrawled across the pages in her diary... Grace picked up the book gently, lov-ingly.

She ran her finger over the painting of the light-house – the lighthouse that was going to save her from misery – the lighthouse that was going to bring a light back into her dark world. How dark her world had become; the light had been shattered, and all she held in her hands was a shard of what once was and could have been.

She felt as if her hands held the last remnant of her broken heart, the one piece of it that was left pumping.

She opened the book to the first page and began to read the words, hoping that somehow these words would give her what she needed to go on, now that everything else in her world was gone...

...

The ocean holds memories... memories that linger in the rising mists, riding the tides as they rise and fall. I've been ridiculed for thinking this before, but I feel almost as if the ocean holds memories of things that I myself haven't seen or done. It holds stories and secrets long forgotten and untold. But still it carries them in its ever-changing currents.

The masses of green and blue water and rising foam drift in a peaceful hush. They whisper of their secrets. When I close my eyes, I can hear them in my head. I can feel the words, though I cannot completely understand them.

The ocean knows me in ways a friend never could...

The ocean holds all of my memories, and the memories of everyone who has come before and who will come hence. Its infinite expanse is home to wandering souls and searching spirits, who, at last, find a friend when they set their eyes upon its shapeless form...

If you search, you never can find where it begins, where it ends, or where it goes. It just is... as some things just are. And it's there for you...

...

Here Grace paused for a moment; she had the ocean, she realized, the same ocean that Charlotte had called her own. She had a friend that kept and stored all of her memories and shared the memories of others as well. She had her very own Ocean of Memories, like the large seashell that Sam had given her. It sat quietly on the dresser. She knew the ocean was inside of it. Somehow, imagining having her own piece of the ocean trapped inside a seashell made her feel comforted.

In the light of the lamp above her bed, Grace continued reading.

...

Dear Diary,

Life has been a fury. Hats and fancy clothes have burned my gaze for too long. Ridiculing eyes and false expectations have grown to weigh heavily upon me. Mother wishes me to be growing into the same sort of civilized being as she is.

But she doesn't understand – truly she doesn't.

I suppose there is too much of Father in me. He being the courageous captain he was.

There is far more to life than pleasing the rich benefactors at fancy parties. There is much more one can do other than sitting around all day doing nothing but small talk. And I don't design to be enwreathed in the folly. Life has a meaning, and it has a truth. And looking pretty should well be below the design of any individual.

For is that not what the flowers do all day? And what think we of them? We trample across them where they sway in the field or pick them and cast them aside.

Don't overlook my design – flowers are beautiful and should never be mistreated, but I feel there is a far greater reason for my own life than to suffer in the destiny of a flower.

So at last I have taken action.

And to my astonishment, Mother consented.

We had been to Mackinac Island before, but never had she let me go with just Claire. It is a gift I will treasure. I do fear this is my last summer like this. As I have turned eighteen, she has tried to inspire me into making friends with the young gentlemen.

But I would rather take the place of their corsage than stand beside them merely to be looked upon. There are trinkets enough to fill the task.

Claire and I have permission to live in our Summer Home, there in Mackinac – the island off of the Philadelphian coast. We had to board a train before we were even able to get to the ocean liner that would carry us across the ocean's expanse.

But it was well worth the trip, belabored as it seemed. I loved watching the forests pass my window on the train. The weather has been beautiful this August. The sun is so bright it lifts the spirit to higher heights.

Sometimes I wish I could drift off on a sunbeam – never again to return.

All the same, our house in Mackinac is a dream. I call it the White House on a Hill. When you stand just outside the gate, it appears to be sitting on a peaceful hill, all its own.

We have a piano here, which I love to play so I can vent my emotions a little.

All the best and more soon...
–Charlotte

...

Dear Diary,

Today I found the oddest thing. A pocket watch! It washed up on the beach. And as I walked along the shores, the tide receded, and there it sat. It gleamed so in the sunlight that my eye couldn't miss it.

It is a strange thing. In the lid there's a strange poem – a riddle of sorts. I call it my "Mackinac Mystery." I've always wanted to figure something out. Maybe I would discover something or unravel a secret. It would be wonderful to have a real adventure during my last summer.

–Charlotte

...

This entry baffled Grace. Though she wasn't sure of it, it seemed that Charlotte was talking about the very same pocket watch Sam had found.

Grace removed it from her pocket and opened the lid.

The engraved words gleamed in the dim light – cold and mysterious.

Suddenly the room lit up with lightning, ripping Grace out of Charlotte's world. She shivered, listening for a moment to the rain as it fell on the roof of her room. She could hear the pitters and patters as they gently lulled her out of her surprise.

Though Grace was beginning to feel tired, she had more to read. She wanted to know more about the watch and more about Charlotte. She opened the book again and read on.

MISSING

When Sam opened his eyes, he wondered if he was dreaming. The last thing he could remember was fainting in the ocean. But here he was, awake and alive. He sat up and stared out at the ocean. His clothes were still damp, and he shivered from the cold air.

But somehow, now he felt all right. The running, and the swimming, and then the fainting, had used up all of his energy, and it had somehow released his fury as well. Now he was calm again, though he could feel that the coldness was piercing deeper than he had expected it to. He could feel it seizing up around his emotions, numbing his heart.

...

By now it was morning, but Grace read on in the diary...

...

Dear Diary,

I find it hard to pen the words to you, for fear I might betray my secret heart.

For the first time in my life, I found someone who understands me. Mother would say Edward doesn't have the proper upbringing, but what does she know?

We met in the park. He was only passing through, but he had to stop and talk. He asked me if I was here for long or short term.

I told him I was only visiting for the summer.

I will admit, his ragged jeans and ratty shirt added to my interest in him – knowing Mother wouldn't approve. But he had a sweet laugh and a gentle smile.

I didn't think much of our meeting, that is, until he searched me out, and I found him on the front porch to our house with a bouquet of daisies. Claire had a good laugh over him from the window, but I ran off with him, and we spent the day together.

He took us to get our pictures taken. I had never had a photograph taken before. They were foreign contraptions to me, but they could work magic – producing a perfect image of Claire, then myself, and then one of him.

Then we went out to the beach and danced while the sun was setting.

He hadn't danced before, so I taught him how. Waltzes are the best, so I taught him one. He is a quick learner.

He surprised me in giving me a locket – with the picture of him in one half and me in the other. It is a treasure to me.

You must promise me, diary, to never rattle my secrets to anyone, for if Edward truly knew how I felt about him after just our few encounters, it would send me into a furious blush.

The secret is ours...

Always,
—Charlotte

...

Edward... Grace thought to herself. She finally knew the name of the long-mysterious face, or at least she thought she did. Edward... she thought again. She wished Charlotte had been obliged to write his last name, but she had obviously been content with only his first name. Grace was baffled. It was another clue that started pouring in the questions...

...

Sam was starving. It was a long walk back to the lighthouse. The sky had stopped raining for a while, though the clouds were still dark and treacherous. Sam thought of his uncle again, wondering where he might be or if he was all right, but he tried not to worry. He tried very hard.

...

Dear Diary,

For shame, August has flitted by like the summer wind. And now it is gone. September has come. And the changing winds of autumn have brought a letter from Mother in Maine with train and boat tickets.

I must obey. I cannot linger, but it is hard to part with everything. I haven't been able to solve the Mack-

inac Mystery, and I'm afraid I will never be able to. I fear this is my last trip as a child. If I return, I return to never look back on my childhood ambitions. I return, like a withered autumn leaf, to the rest of my life in high society with fancy hats and high collars.

If I could, I would throw it all away.

You know my heart. I want to stay here with Edward. I love him. And unless my hopes are leading me beyond sanity, I believe he loves me, too.

What will he say when I tell him I must leave?

I don't even want to know.

That is why I will leave him a message on the door. It is my final farewell. For in truth, I am never coming back to Mackinac. All of this is left behind with the leaving of the ocean liner.

I apologize for the tears on your perfect pages, dear diary, but I cannot keep them back. Why did I ever have to love someone I could never really have?

I feel as if I belong to the wrong shores...

But as Elizabeth says in Jane Austin's masterpiece: "Think only of the past as its remembrance gives you pleasure..."

That is what I will tell Edward. And I will leave my good friend, my book Pride and Prejudice. He says he has never read it. So I will leave it for him.

I pray he will understand that I must go – it is not a choice.

Regretfully,
–Charlotte

...

The tears were welling up in Grace's eyes as she read Charlotte's account. Grace had lost people she loved dearly. She started to think of her parting with Sam... but Grace spent little time thinking of this. There was more, still, to read.

...

Dear Diary,

I am weeping now like a child. And I'm here on the ocean liner, in front of the masses of people. But it doesn't matter. The tears I cannot hold back.

My message was designed to keep myself from facing Edward's goodbye, but it was a deed done in vain...

I was going to throw the pocket watch back into the ocean, where it belonged, but he came before I could bring myself to do it.

He found me on the port before I boarded the ocean liner. I hugged him, telling him I would stay if I could. He didn't say anything. He just stared into the distance, at the ocean. And then I knew that he didn't want me to leave either. But he knew it wouldn't help if he showed it; he couldn't tell me because admitting that he felt the same way I did would make it harder for him to let go and harder for me to leave.

But by not saying anything, he said it all. And perhaps more.

I held back most of my tears, but some escaped.

I suddenly gave him the pocket watch. The legend needed to stay with the island. I couldn't steal it from its home. I had to leave it all behind. I didn't have time to explain what it was, but I told him it was his now.

Then I turned and hurried onto the boat.

Standing on the deck, I waved at him, but he didn't wave back. He never waved back. He just stood there looking at me... seeing right through me. I will never forget the image of him – it's burned into my mind.

Both of his hands were in his pockets, his head slightly slumped. His mouth held no expression. But his eyes! His eyes said everything. They were much deeper than the ocean itself. And though they were so close, they were so distant. So far away... I could see so far into them, I almost became hopelessly lost. But the ship carried me away.

I crumbled before he was even out of sight. The tears were too much for me. Claire tried to comfort me, but nothing will soothe this ache. Nothing.

In my heart, I felt as if I had hurt him. He had loved me and trusted me with his love. And then I had to leave. And though I was more sorry than I could ever be, he seemed unable to tell.

He stood like a cold pillar in the face of a storm.

I don't know how life will go on. I just don't know...

You are my only hope to survival, my dear, my sweet book. You let me explain everything. Thank you. If I didn't have a silent friend like you, I don't know where I would be.

Your Confidant,
–Charlotte

THE SEARCH

Grace was weeping like a child now, her hand covering her mouth. She tried not to cry, but the tears fell with no control or direction. They just flowed like a river from her broken heart. Why is it when you love someone that they have to be taken away? Grace had loved her parents – they were dead. She had loved Sam – he was gone.

Now she didn't know who was left to love.

Her aunt was still the same, cold person she had been for sixty years. Over many years, cold hearts seize up. It takes more than a warm day to melt them – it takes something jolting, something that will break the ice all the way down to the core. To Grace, it seemed like it would take something that almost reopened the wounds that had been iced over because frozen wounds aren't really healed.

...

Sam lay on his bed, staring out the window. The book <u>Pride and Prejudice</u> sat on the stand next to him. He picked it up and hurled it across the room. In the far corner it lay like a wounded bird, sprawled out with the pages curled beneath it.

Sam felt a twinge of guilt for a moment, and then he walked across the room and picked it up carefully. He was beginning to wonder what was wrong with him. Since Grace had left, he hadn't been himself.

His anger had more control over him than his patience or even his wits. He had nearly drowned because he was angry. He was angry at Grace's aunt, but he realized he was punishing himself and Grace as well.

And then he realized something else. His uncle had been gone for three days. The storms had been raging for two. It had been too long. As the realization sank in deeper he wondered. Was this day the day that his uncle had always spoken about? The day that he would leave and never return? Sam could feel his eyes beginning to sting.

"No!" His uncle couldn't leave. Not yet. Not like this.

Sam pulled on his coat and boots and left the lighthouse – he had to get help. Before it was too late. He thought grimly that already, it probably was too late...

...

Grace lay on her pillow for a moment, letting the tears run free. She watched from her window as a gentle rain began to fall again. She wanted to run out in it and cry, but she felt confined to her room. She knew that all her aunt wanted was for her to forget about everything that had happened.

This made Grace laugh. She wouldn't forget, ever. She could never forget about something that had been so wonderful and so exciting as her days with Sam had been. It was impossible to forget.

Then Grace recognized something else. Her aunt had tried to build over the top of her pain – this was why she could laugh sometimes. This was how she could keep living, but the distance was the pain that still pricked, the pain that drew her eyes to the ocean.

Grace wished she could completely understand.

She turned back to the diary. Her only clue was the diary. She hoped it said what Grace needed to know... but she could only hope...

...

Dear Diary,

It's the rainy season here in Maine. The sky never seems to clear. The rain always falls. I have found a new favorite thing to do. I love to cry in the rain. I cry for the summer that is gone that will never return.

Crying is all I do now. It's all I can do.

Life with a broken heart is no life at all. It's an empty shell without the pearl.

Mother wonders what is wrong with me, but I don't even try to explain. I can't even begin to. Claire understands a little. But I wish she could understand better.

I have no desire for words.

These thin, scrawled words have no life. I have no life to give to them and them none to me.

I'm lonely, though there are hoards of crowds and people; I'm all alone. My loneliness is for the one who I can never see, who I can never love.

Sometimes I imagine his ship, sailing into the port. Or I see him out of the corner of my eye. But he's never there.

—Charlotte

...

The first place Sam went was to talk to Captain Grey.

"I haven't seen him – his boat isn't in the pier," Grey had said.

"Do you have any idea where he might be?" Sam pressed.

Grey shrugged. "I've heard him talk about his secret fishing hole before, but he's never taken me there."

"Who would know where it is? I'm worried something bad has happened to him."

Grey nodded solemnly, "I haven't seen any fishing boat live through a storm like this one's been..."

"Are you telling me you think he's gone... dead?"

Grey nodded solemnly. "Going out in a storm like that isn't a wise thing. He's had a boat go down before, you know."

Sam had never heard that story before. Really, he didn't know much to anything about his uncle. They never talked about his past, or his friends, or family. He only had Sam, and Sam only had him.

"No..." Sam said. "He can't be dead!"

Sam burst from Captain Grey's cabin. He wanted to run off down the beach again, but he knew that he had to do something to help. His mind was racing with thoughts. He was so worried he couldn't think straight. His thoughts were jumbled together with frightening questions. Could his uncle really be gone? What would happen if he was? Would Sam have to go to an orphanage? Who would take over the lighthouse?

It was all very frightening, and with his thoughts racing, he couldn't think of anything sensible to do.

Suddenly Grey was behind him. He placed a large hand on Sam's shoulder and said, "We should call together a search party. The police need to know, and the coast guard might be helpful, too."

"Do you really think he's gone?"

Grey stared at the sky for a moment. Then he said, "All we can do is hope that he's not."

...

It took Grace a moment before she could read any more. She hadn't realized that anyone's life could be so difficult. It seemed like Charlotte would have understood exactly what Grace was going through. They could have at least cried together and comforted each other a little.

For just a moment, Grace imagined that they were together. The journal was like a portal of time, bringing them together across the span of history.

When Grace gained her composure again, she opened the book and read on...

...

Dear Diary,

Today I happened upon a message in a bottle. I must have a knack for running into random articles of garbage that have washed up along the shores.

But this was no piece of trash... there was a poem inside of the bottle. I don't know who wrote it or where it came from. I promise it was written for me.

Come away,
Come away to the ocean my weary friend,
We'll travel the seas together.
I know you're lost and alone,
But leave the weathered stone.
Don't yourself smolder in unfamiliar shores...
Come away,
I'll take you away,
You know your rightful home...

Whoever penned the words must have felt what my heart felt. And it causes me to wonder – did they come away? Did they go off with the ocean, leaving fears and worries behind. And all of this, did they do for the sake of a brighter dream?

I don't know. And I can't know.

But what I can know is whether or not I will heed the message.

I've been crying in the rain for what seems like years. And the tears have left no stain. Tears dry, and time goes on. I can't change the future by mourning over the past.

But I can change the future because of the past.

And I will. I trust my heart more than my eyes. I trust my joy and heed my pain. My love, my heart, I have left in a distant shore. And without it, I am no longer myself.

September and October have felt like years of endless solitude. I am tired of being alone. If I belonged here, I would understand things better. But I don't. And I never have belonged here.

So now, I will reunite...

Thank you, Unknown Author – you are truly my friend. May your ship sail you down peaceful waters.

I added a message to the bottle, and tossed it back out to see...

And I will return to Mackinac.

In fact, I'm running away...

Message in a Bottle

Sam watched as the Coast Guard's boat sailed into the distance. The sky was still overcast, but no rain had fallen. Sam was hopeful that they would be able to continue the search.

Captain Grey had set sail in his own fishing boat, going the other direction to search. He had told Sam before he left, "It looks like a storm is coming. As soon as it starts raining it's going to be too dangerous to continue searching; we're going to have to head back."

"But we can't stop until we find my uncle," Sam pressed.

"If we stay on the water in this weather, we're all dead..." Grey's voice rumbled with the authority of many years' experience.

Sam nodded solemnly. He was left with the ground crew, to search along the shores. The police had gathered together a squad to search the cliffs and beaches. Everyone had fanned out and each had an area to search. Sam was all by himself, and so he had some good time to think.

He stared at the ground, kicking loose pebbles around. Inside, his stomach was churning. He worried that any moment the horrible news would come. He wanted it all to end; he wanted to know where his uncle was. But at the same time, he wanted the truth to stay away for as long as it could be held off because he didn't want to face the horrible truth.

...

Grace hadn't been able to put the diary down after reading the last entry. She was amazed with Charlotte's courage. She had run away from her family and her parents, all for the one she loved. It was a bold thing to do. Grace wondered if she could ever be that brave...

...

Dear Diary,

I've never been so scared in my life. It was dark the night that Claire and I ran away. I've never done anything so sneaky in my life, but some things must be done.

Claire and I had to pull together our savings in order to afford the bus and boat tickets, but we were able to do so, with even a little to spare.

I will probably have to get a job in Mackinac, but that will be all right – everything is going to be all right now. I just know it will... I know it will.

–Charlotte

...

Dear Diary,

The Island is a different place in November. I've never seen the trees so empty. The little streets are bordered with fallen leaves. It's a stark but beautiful sight. It's cold – jacket weather. I prefer the island in summer, but autumn has an appeal I can't deny.

When the ocean liner pulled into the port, I cried because of how wonderful it felt to be home.

I found Edward at the lighthouse. He was in the watch, just staring out. When he saw Claire and me coming down the hill, somehow he knew it was I.

He ran down all of the steps in the tower, picking me up and swinging me around when he reached me at last.

He told me that he had kept the lighthouse burning for me, praying that I would return. I told him about the message in the bottle, and that I had run away. Then his eyes sparkled playfully.

He told me that he had been searching for the item that the pocket watch had spoken of. He thinks that the forgotten cove is an underwater cove, one that is completely underwater... in other words, he thinks he knows where the silver pearl is! If he truly knows this, Claire and I can survive comfortably on the Island.

How I hope it's true! Life has returned to what it was before, and what I hope it will always remain!

Forever,
—Charlotte

...

What did Charlotte mean? She had talked about the silver pearl. This meant that she, in fact, had found the same pocket watch that Sam had found. Grace wondered why Sam had found the watch out in the ocean. Obviously it had been lost somehow, somewhere near the lighthouse. Now she wondered if they had found the pearl. If Edward knew where the silver pearl was... The more Charlotte talked about Edward, the more Grace felt like she knew him. Or at least, the more she felt like she should know him.

But Grace was suddenly afraid to read on. She was unsure whether or not she wanted to read the next entry because it was the last one. It filled several of the small journal pages, but it was all that was left.

For a few minutes, Grace bit her lip as she debated. At last she started reading again, hoping almost hopelessly, that somehow she would be able to find the answers to her questions in this final entry...

...

Dear Diary,

This is my last entry to you, and I tell you all will end happily. Edward knows where the silver pearl is hidden. He's known the place all of his life. In fact, he says it's what he calls his 'Secret Fishing Hole'. So we're going fishing – Edward, Claire, and I. We haven't told Claire about the silver pearl; we thought it would be best if she didn't know about it until we found it. She's never been one to believe in anything that seems too good to be true.

My sister is the more practical one out of the two of us, but I love her for it. She's what every big sister should be. We told her we were going fishing today. She's a little skeptical of it, as the sky is overcast. However, I soon won her over to the idea with my smiles and enthusiasm.

But now, my dear diary... I've been thinking about you. I have reached the final pages in your cover and it seems as if it is time to say goodbye. You have been such a friend through all of this, and now it's time for us to part. For some unknown reason, I don't feel like I will need to read through your pages again.

Now I want to hide away all of my secrets inside of you. I want to keep you somewhere safe. I feel like I should hide you away and do something mysterious!

No, my friend, don't fear! I won't shut you away to never be seen again. For what purpose is a book, but to be read? Instead, I will hide you in a very safe place in the lighthouse. I will leave a trail of clues that lead to finding you. This way, you will not be lost; you'll be preserved.

I am using all of my best tricks to hide you and create the clues, so that only the person that is meant to find you, will. I know that special person won't abuse you.

I must, though, share one last secret with you. My very most favorite of secrets... Edward proposed to me yesterday. I haven't told Clarenne yet, but he wants to marry me! Of course, I gave him my consent. He says a wedding in spring would be lovely... I agree!

Fare thee well, my friend,

I will never forget you,

And you, I know, will never forget me...

Across the ages,
—Charlotte

...

After reading these words, Grace broke down sobbing. She knew what had happened next. She knew the whole story, though the details weren't confirmed. Her heart was throbbing in agony. Suddenly she understood why the portrait of Charlotte was in the basement – to be forgotten.

Grace understood, now, that the boat trip Charlotte spoke of in her final diary entry was in fact the very same trip that had claimed her life. She had looked at it as being a glorious adventure, and she had been so happy before she died...

Everything had fallen into place for Grace when she had read that 'Claire', Charlotte's sister, had the full name "Clarenne". She was Clarenne Happs, her own aunt. Charlotte was Clarenne's younger sister.

...

As he walked along the shore, Sam realized he hadn't been on this part of the island before. In the distance he could see something glimmering on the shore. And first he wondered what it might be, but as he got closer, he realized it was nothing but an old bottle.

Sam was beginning to feel frustrated about everything. He felt discouraged, and he worried that there was nothing left to hope for. He picked up the bottle and cocked his arm back to throw it out into the ocean, but as he lifted it, he saw something move inside.

Then Sam wiped off the sand and mud that was caked on the outside of the bottle. He realized that there was a roll of paper inside the bottle, a message. It was a message in a bottle.

Sam patiently undid the cork in the bottle. It was pressed in firmly, so as not to let any water into the bottle, and it had done its job well. When Sam tipped the bottle and shook it upside-down, a skinny roll of yellowed paper slid into his hand.

It was tied with a piece of yarn. Sam slid this off carefully.

He unrolled the paper gingerly. It was so old that it crinkled and it seemed like it would easily rip. There were actually two papers inside the bundle. One was so old and ragged it was nearly brown, but the second was far newer, although it too seemed very old.

On the first page, the newer one, was a scribbled message...

> *Life is weary when it's lived alone...*
> *Never make the same mistake*
> *And leave the one you love...*
> *For life without love is none to own.*
> *But, I pray it's not too late...*
> *Return – for your love cannot wait...*

The second, older page read:

> *Come away,*

Come away to the ocean my weary friend;
We'll travel the seas together.
I know you're lost and alone,
But leave the weathered stone;
Don't yourself smolder in unfamiliar shores...
Come away,
I'll take you away,
You know your rightful home...

Sam knew the poems were talking to him. They were telling him what he needed to do. He knew that he must face Grace's aunt. He knew he loved Grace, though he didn't want to outwardly admit it; he knew that he did.

Suddenly the wind stole one of the pages, carrying it away down the beach. Sam hurried after it, snatching it up before it flew off and was lost forever to the ocean.

And when he picked it up, he realized that there was a second message on the back of the newer page. It had been written in pencil, fading and almost unreadable...

Edward Warner, my love, I'm coming back to you...
—Charlotte

Sam paled as he read this, and then he hit himself on the head. How could he have been so naïve? And even worse, how could he have been so unobservant? Sam knew who was in the other picture in the locket. He had known all along. It was the one person that he knew better than anyone else, the one he hoped to find...

It was Edward, Sam's uncle...

CHARLOTTE

Still trying to fully recover from her surprise, Grace sat on her bed, listening to silence. And then suddenly she knew what to do. She picked up the diary and left her room. Her heart was racing – she knew that this wasn't going to be easy, but it was time to break her aunt's cold heart – time for her to face the feelings she had buried for so long now.

Down the stairs, upon entering the kitchen, Grace saw her aunt sitting at the table. Her face was full of color as she smiled at Grace.

"Hello, Grace, my dear..."

Grace didn't say anything, but held the book out in front of her so that Clarenne could see the cover.

Suddenly her aunt's face paled. "Where did you get that?" she whispered.

"That doesn't matter. I deserve an explanation. You have forbid me from talking to someone, and I cannot do that until I have a decent explanation."

"No... Grace. Everything happened too long ago. It was too long ago to matter anymore."

"Then why are you holding on to it as if it happened yesterday?"

"You don't understand," Clarenne sobbed.

"Then help me understand..." Grace sat down at the table. She pulled the locket out from where it had been hiding and held it out for Clarenne to see. "I know a lot of things—a lot more than you think. I just want to know what happened... the day she died."

Clarenne covered her face and sobbed for a moment. She rocked back and forth, trying to comfort herself. "Lottie, oh Lottie—what have I done? Whatever have I done?" She wept, forgetting Grace for a moment.

Grace began to despair, wondering if she could ever break through to her aunt.

But slowly Clarenne took her hands from her face, staring out the window behind Grace. Without taking her gaze from the drifting waves she said, "You know, this is the first time I really cried over her... I felt so bad. So sorry—but I knew it was all my fault. I shouldn't have let them go. I shouldn't have. But I did. I even went, too. And if I hadn't, Edward would have been able to save Lottie, but no, he had to save me first..."

Still staring out the window, Grace could see the years peeling away from her memory as she drifted back to the moment. Clarenne smiled weakly for a moment, and then she began...

...

It was a cold autumn day when we returned to the island. Lottie and I had run away from home, and it seemed to be the most dangerous thing we could have done. But at the same time, we both knew it was right.

I had known that Lottie loved Edward – I had seen her tears, understanding how it hurt to miss him. And though I hoped it would somehow mend, I knew it was true love – for true love is the only love that makes you hurt like she hurt.

It pained me to see her cry, though I never wept the same tears. I never cried much, but she did. She cried every night for her Edward, holding her locket in her hands, gazing at his picture under candlelight.

But then the night came when she told me her plan. I didn't want her to do it, but at the same time, I knew that she had to. She had left her heart on this island... and she would never be able to find it anywhere else.

So we took the midnight train and boarded the ocean liner, and soon enough we arrived on Mackinac Island.

Lottie took off running as soon as the boat docked. I had to hurry to keep up with her. Her hat fell back, bouncing behind her as she ran. Both of our dresses were long, proper dresses, so it made it difficult to run, but Lottie seemed to fly across the beach like a seagull who had been freed at last from a horrible cage.

Edward saw us coming, and he met Lottie in the sand. He swung her around. Then they just stood there, looking at each other. Lottie never knew how happy it made me feel to see her smile again.

The Lottie I had loved had disappeared for the months we had returned to Maine, but now I had finally found her again, and I was happier than I could ever be. All I wanted was this to remain as it was now. All I wanted was for Lottie to be happy with Edward.

But things didn't stay that way...

Mother wrote a letter a couple days after we had arrived at the island. She was worried, and she wanted to know if we were all right. I had kept the letter from Lottie so that she wouldn't be worried over it.

It wasn't many days later that she told me about her and Edward's plan to go on a fishing trip – to Edward's secret fishing hole. It sounded exciting, and Lottie seemed a little secretive about it all. I felt as if there were some secrets that she was keeping from me. Though in her eyes, I could see the promise that she would tell me about them soon enough.

I was worried about the weather. I had the gut-feeling that we should stay and wait until it wasn't a stormy day, but Lottie said that she and Edward were going – I could stay home if I liked. Of course I couldn't do that, and I was dying to know of Lottie's secrets, so I went along.

Everything was all right for a while. She and Edward laughed and talked as the boat set sail. Then they threw something shimmering off the side of the boat—which I thought was odd. I asked Lottie what it was, and she said that it was just a pocket watch they didn't need any more.

Edward took the boat around strange cliffs and turns. He said we were almost there when it started to rain. Before we could turn around or do anything, the storm was upon us. It was raining so hard. Within moments the ocean, which had been calm, had raging tidal waves. The winds whipped across the ocean, building the waves taller and stronger.

We tried to turn the boat around. We left the cove safely. We even came close enough to the shore that we could see it again. But by now, the storm was so strong Edward could hardly control the boat.

The waves thrust the boat against a rock. At first we had thought everything was all right. That is, until the boat started sinking. We had to jump off of the boat into the raging waves. I have never been so terrified in my life.

For a moment I kept above the water, until a wave came and thrust me under. Suddenly I was lost in the darkness. Below, everything was peaceful. Though I couldn't find my way to the surface, it was peaceful.

Then Edward grabbed me and pulled me to the surface again. I tried to stay above, but the waves buried me. I was a swimmer, but not in that sort of waves. I told Edward to let me be and to help Lottie, but he insisted to help me first. He had to help me until I was almost ashore. When I could manage the rest of the way, he told me to get help.

I ran as fast as I could to Captain Grey's pier. I told him we needed help, and he brought out a boat. We looked for Edward for a while – a long while. We finally found him afloat on the tide. Grey pulled him into the boat. He was unconscious, but Grey pushed on his chest until gasped and revived.

"Lottie... Lottie..." he called.

But she wasn't there. We searched the ocean for hours—the cold, boat lights on the black ocean turning this way and that. Edward called again and again, but there was never an answer.

Never an answer.

We don't really know what happened to her. I would never forgive myself - I should have never let them go. But I also could never forgive Edward because he should have gone back for Lottie and left me to the waves. I would have been the one who died, and Lottie would still be alive...

...

Grace understood now. She understood it all, and now both Clarenne and Grace wept without control, though Clarenne wept harder.

"My mother came to the island for the funeral – disowning me entirely. She never spoke a word. I could tell that she blamed me for my sister's death as well. If I wouldn't have consented to Lottie's plan to escape, she would have died from a broken heart..." Clarenne muttered through her tears.

"But instead, she died happily..." Grace said comfortingly. "And that was *because* you agreed."

"I could never speak to Edward again because I knew that he would disown me as well... that he would blame me for Lottie's death. So I lived alone. I had no friends on the island, and I never felt like searching people out. The ocean became my only friend. Looking into it, I could find Lottie there..." Clarenne stared out the window again.

"But now you have a friend..."

Grace hugged Clarenne. For a moment her aunt hesitated, and then she consented, returning the hug completely.

"I'm sorry, my dear," she whispered. "For being so selfish..."

Grace didn't know what to say, but she knew that her aunt was the old Clarenne again—the one that Charlotte would want her to be.

Suddenly the door burst open. It was pouring rain outside, and there was Sam in the doorway.

"I'm really sorry, Miss Happs..." he said. "But I *need* your help."

"Sam!" Grace said.

"What is it, boy?" Clarenne asked.

"My uncle is out in the storm... I think you might know where he is. I think you're the only one."

"Edward?" Clarenne asked.

"Your uncle?" Grace asked suddenly. "Edward... is your *uncle*?"

"We have no time to discuss the past any further right now, Grace." Clarenne got up and pulled on her coat and boots. "You're right; I think I do know where your uncle is."

Remembering

Clarenne took Sam and Grace to the pier in the Chevy. All the while, Grace explained the story to Sam – she told him about what she had read in Charlotte's diary and about what her aunt had said.

Sam told Grace that he had found the message in a bottle on the beach.

Soon they reached the pier. The windshield wipers were racing madly in order to keep up with the rain that fell, and they all knew that they had to soon go out in the horrible storm. They stopped on the pier. Clarenne turned the car's headlights off, and they just sat there for a moment in the rain.

"I can't believe I'm about to commit to this," Clarenne said. "After all that I've been through..." She held out one hand to Sam and the other to Grace. "But I think this is the only way I can ever repay your uncle."

"Let's do it," Sam said.

...

Captain Grey's boat was at the pier already. They had stopped searching as he had promised – when the rain had started. Grace went with Sam into the cabin to talk to Grey.

"It's all over," Grey said. "There is no way you're going to find Edward. I'm sorry, but we have to just admit he's gone."

With that, Sam fell to his knees covering his face. "He can't be gone," Sam cried.

Really it was all an act, but it was so convincing Grace almost fell for it and believed that Sam had given up, but then she remembered what she had to do.

Grey knelt next to Sam with a hand on his shoulder. "It'll be all right, son. I'll make sure you're taken care of..."

Grace went to the pegboard where the keys for all of the boats were kept. She found the one with the number that Sam had told her to get, and she pulled it off of the peg and slid it into her pocket. They weren't stealing the boat – just borrowing it.

Next, Grace quietly left the cabin, seeming to leave out of respect to Sam.

Outside the cabin, she and Clarenne hurried to the port and climbed into the boat.

"I haven't done this for forever," Clarenne whispered excitedly.

She turned the key and the boat roared to a start.

When Sam heard the boat start up, he knew the signal. Suddenly he jumped up from where he had been kneeling and burst out of the cabin door, which Grace had left slightly ajar. He ran straight down the deck for the fishing boat that Clarenne had pulled up at the end of the dock.

It was a several foot distance between the dock and the boat, but Sam cleared it with precision.

"What's going on?" Grey yelled from the doorway of his cabin.

But they were already gone.

Once Sam took over the driving of the boat, he revved up the motor and the little boat sped across the water. The waves weren't very high in this part of the ocean, but Sam knew that as they got closer to the cliffs that they would have to be cautious – a lot more cautious.

It was a long and winding route that Clarenne led them on. Sam only hoped that she remembered the way.

Her brow was furrowed in thought. Sometimes she remembered only barely in time for him to lurch between the rocks. There were many rocks to steer around and crevices between cliffs to enter. Every now and again there were long expanses of water between and everything was silent.

Grace stood next to Sam, silently debating whether or not she should tell him about the silver pearl. She knew that they were going to the exact place where the forgotten cove was that had been talked about on the pocket watch. It was hard for her to forget about it. Though she knew that this was no time to be treasure hunting, she wondered if they might have an opportunity to just look.

Because she knew how badly Charlotte had wanted to find the pearl, she almost felt like it was her duty to fulfill Charlotte's dream and find the silver pearl, but then again, she also knew that it wasn't worth risking her life over.

Grace had the pocket watch in her pocket. She felt its cold surface with her hand. Looking up at Sam, she could see his face, intent on steering the boat. There at the stern of the boat, she could feel the wind in her face. Though it was raining down on her, she loved the peace in the rain, even though there was a threat, Grace knew, on all of their lives.

She shivered all of a sudden, wondering if she, herself, would come back alive. She looked at Sam and smiled. This was, perhaps, her last smile to him, and there in the whole of the moment, she decided that it was all right if she died. She was happy at last. Happy that Clarenne had forgiven Edward, and more importantly, she had forgiven herself. Grace felt like she had done what Lottie would have wanted her to do had she herself been there.

In Grace's heart, she was letting go...

As the boat came closer and closer to Edward's secret fishing hole, the waves became more and more treacherous. Every now and again, the boat would rock so tremendously that it seemed it would capsize at any moment, but somehow it always stayed right side up.

Sam was determined to bring all of them home safely. He was determined to find his uncle and determined to set everything right, more right than it had been even before. But Sam didn't know his fate, and he didn't know the fate of those who he brought with him. He didn't even know the fate of his uncle or if his uncle was still alive. This whole brigade could all be a false hope. For at any second, fate could turn its cold hand against him, and he could lose. He could lose everything...

Clarenne's mind was reeling back as if this route was a portal through time for her. It was almost as if she were going to see her sister again, but she knew that it was a foolish thing to believe. She was here to save Edward. Lottie would want him to live, and Lottie would want her to forgive Edward. Clarenne couldn't remember the way to the fishing hole. Seeing it but once, she had no way of knowing for sure, but it seemed as if her memory had been sharpened and that a warm hand was resting on her shoulder. It felt like her sister was there with her – guiding her every step and turn.

They came to an opening between two cliffs and turned in between them. This was a dangerous area with cliffs on either side of them. It was a long, narrow stretch of water, and when they came to the end, there was another opening that led to a large area of open water.

"This is it..." Clarenne said. "This is Edward's secret fishing hole. We're here..."

THE FORGOTTEN COVE

Just then a large wave rushed in from the ocean, rocking the boat so furiously, it again almost capsized. Sam turned off the motor of the boat and called for his uncle.

In response, a rattling sound came from the far side of the cove. Sam turned one of the boat's headlights towards the sound and almost fainted.

There, battered and broken was his uncle's boat.

"Uncle!" Sam yelled.

It was a horrible sight to see. The boat was in such shambles it could hardly be a boat.

"Sam... I'm afraid he really is gone," Clarenne choked on the words.

"No!" Sam yelled.

He took several steps backwards on the boat, and then flung himself over the edge. He flew several feet into the air and fell into the roaring waves.

"Sam!" Grace screamed. Tears gathered in her eyes, coming together and falling harder than the rain that poured down. "Sam... you can't! You can't go!" she screamed.

Clarenne was at her side, holding her close.

"Come back! Please come back!" she wailed.

But Sam was too deep in the water to hear her words as they echoed across the water, bouncing off of the cliff walls. All of the echoed voices came back to her, cold and forbidding. They seemed to mock her pain. Grace grabbed Clarenne closer and sobbed into her shoulder.

...

Sam had seen a cave on the far side of the shore. It wasn't far from the boat wreckage, and Sam had a fool's hope that his uncle could possibly be alive – in there.

He fought the current, pushing his way towards the far shore. It was a fight he almost couldn't win. The tides and roaring water surrounded him, screaming in his ears. The waves covered him, crashing over the top of him again and again.

Really he should have given up. It was all hopeless, but there was one last, little light burning in Sam's heart. It was like a lighthouse that had burned down to embers, and though it wasn't much, it was just enough to keep him fighting the current that tried so hard to stop him—tried so hard to bury him.

Soon enough, when he was almost ready to give up, he reached the rock wall and pulled himself onto the ledge – to the mouth of the cave. It was deep, and he couldn't see through to the back, but there were several inches of water on the floor of the cave, and the water level, Sam noted, was rising.

Tramping through the water, splashing as he went, he made his way deeper into the cave. He had no light, and all he could hear was the sound of his own footsteps and water trickling into the cave. "Uncle?" he called. His voice circled around him, echoing back from the walls that surrounded him.

He had taken many steps into the cave when he heard a slight groan, "Sam?"

"It's you!" Sam said. He rushed forward. Though he couldn't see anything, he could hear his uncle moving faintly. "I knew you were alive..."

"Fools hope," his uncle said hoarsely, ruffling Sam's hair. "You shouldn't have come for me. It's a terrible storm out there, and I'm just an old flea bag – not worth risking your young life over."

"Are you all right?"

"I'm in one piece if that's what you want to know, but I think I broke my leg, and I'm hungry as heck. The tide is coming in though, Sam. This whole place is going to be filled with water in a couple minutes."

"I have to get you out of here," Sam said.

With that, he pulled his uncle up. He had to half carry him, as Edward's leg was broken. Their progress was slow, but soon they could see the light at the end of the cave.

"It's a good thing you came, Sam. I don't think I would have been able to hold out much longer."

"What happened?"

"My boat capsized, and a tide smashed me up against the cliff wall. I had to swim with one leg in order to get into this cave, and that was no easy task. After that, I was all right for a while, until the water started rising in here. I had to move deeper into the cave where it got higher." Here Edward groaned again.

"You're going to be all right," Sam said. "We just have to get you to the boat. Grace and Clarenne are waiting for us."

"Clarenne? A lot happened while I was gone..."

"She was the only one who knew where you went – why did you leave like that, and with a storm coming?"

His uncle was silent for a moment. "Well, I had to get away, and I guessed that you and Grace would be hanging out more, so I figured it would be better if I was gone for a while, as I was the reason Grace was forbidden from talking to you, so I thought I might as well take a vacation. Then the storm came, and it was a lot worse than I had anticipated it to be. You know, I'm not too good at reading the weather."

Sam hadn't realized that his uncle had left everything for him and Grace... and suddenly he began to see this other side of his uncle.

His uncle had always been one to keep to himself, not mentioning much about his past, or really anything. But now that he knew a little of what his uncle had been through, Sam began to discover a whole new appreciation for his uncle. And the whole experience of being without him, forced him to imagine what it would be like if he had to live without his uncle... all of it made him grateful to have his uncle there with him.

Soon they would all be home, and everything would be better than it had been before. Sam looked forward to telling his uncle about the message in the bottle and about the diary they had found. He wanted to tell his uncle about it all.

But as they reached the mouth of the cave, Sam realized something wasn't right. What had seemed like such a simple rescue was suddenly turning into a failed attempt that would claim all of their lives.

The boat that had been waiting in the cove, was capsized and both Grace and Clarenne were nowhere in sight.

"No!" Sam yelled.

Leaving his uncle at the mouth of the cave, he dove back into the water. Feelings of regret rushed over him as he splashed in the water. This was his fault. If it weren't for him, none of this would have happened. Grace would be fine with her aunt. His uncle wouldn't have left on the fishing trip, and none of them would have had to come to save him. Everything would have been much, much better if it hadn't been for him.

Grace would have been better off without him...

SHIPWRECK

It hadn't been long after Sam had vanished beneath the black currents that a tidal wave had come around the corner. It was a monster of a wave, and the poor, little fishing boat that Grace and Clarenne had been waiting safely on was lifted high above the regular sea level. Then it had crashed back down again.

Of course the boat tipped over, dumping Grace, Clarenne, and all of the boat's supplies into the water. The boat was sinking fast, and Clarenne tried her best to swim away from it, so as not to be caught in its downward pull. She made it a fair distance away and fought to get her head above the water. Briefly, she caught a glimpse of Sam and his uncle at the mouth of the cave. She tried to scream for help, but another tide came crashing in over her head. The storm wasn't letting up. In fact, it was only growing in its fury.

With her head below the water, everything became suddenly familiar – in the horribly silent calmness that came when one was beneath the water during a storm. She knew this feeling better than she wanted to. It was a feeling she had hoped to never feel again, and the silence that she remembered from so long ago filled her with such overwhelming fear, she froze – unable to move.

It was all over she realized. Her hope of going home and living the same life she had before, it was all over. Even as the feeling of despair hit her, inside her heart she knew that it was all right. The bitter heart that she had carried for so many years was gone. She didn't even sorrow over the risk she had taken to save Edward. She had been so rude to him, when he, in fact, had saved her life. The one thing she wished for, was that she could tell him she was sorry... that she could talk to him one more time...

Suddenly, she could see a dark figure coming towards her. It grabbed her arm and pulled her up to the surface. She gasped for air. Then with its help, she made her way to the cave in the side of the cliff. Coughing, she sat in the water that had collected there. It was now nearly a foot deep.

But there, sitting beside her was Edward.

"Edward..." she whispered. She hurried over and hugged him tightly. "I'm so, so sorry for how I have been these past many years..."

"It hurts to lose the one you love... it really does," Edward's words seemed distant and understanding. Then he looked right at Clarenne, his eyes sparkling dismally. "But it hurts even worse to live with someone you used to care about, feeling like they could never forgive you. Then you have your own shame and the shame of another on your heart, and that makes it almost impossible to go on."

"I'm so sorry..." she said. "Is it too late for us to make amends?"

"It is never too late..." he said.

Just then Sam's voice echoed from the cove, "Grace!" he called. "Grace, where are you?"

But there was no response.

Sam searched frantically, swimming around the boat and then coming back to the surface again; he called her name again and again. Each time he did this, his voice became more and more earnest. Tears were blinding him now, blinding him and stinging his eyes like the saltwater.

Sam hadn't expected this – he hadn't even anticipated this. He should have made Grace stay on the island. Everything would have been better. But no, he had let her come along. It was as if everything was happening in the cycle. Historians that study history for thousands of years, say that history repeats itself, and here it was happening again. History was repeating...

Clarenne was sobbing from the cave, realizing that Grace was gone. "Just when she had helped me so. Just when I was bringing her into my heart, and she was beginning to fill the hole in my heart that had been empty since Lottie died... just when..." she buried her face in Edward's shoulder and he put a gentle arm around her.

"Grace!" Sam shrieked in desperation.

But again, the only response was his echoing voice off the walls of the cliffs – afraid and earnest.

His heart was pounding and his breaths were becoming more and more scarce. His stomach was cramped, and he could feel himself growing more and more tired. But Sam knew there were more places to check. He knew that there was only a little time before it was too late.

Sam swam down to the ocean floor. He swam around the sinking boat. It was so dark now; he couldn't see anything but the mass of the boat. If Grace was trapped, he couldn't see her.

Then, in the small window of the cabin, Sam could see something flapping. It was Grace. She was pounding the window – trying to get away. She was trapped in the lower deck!

Sam hurried to the window and began pounding it with all of the energy he could exert, but it wasn't enough. He was wasted. The little light that had been burning inside of him was fading fast. Soon he could feel himself going limp. Then the tapping inside the cabin stopped.

Grace was gone...

THE GROTTO

When the boat had capsized, and Grace and Clarenne had fallen into the water, Grace had been on the lower end, and she had been thrust deeper into the water than Clarenne had. The boat had hit her arm, and now it was throbbing from the impact of her fall. Grace was below the boat and she knew that if she didn't act fast, she would be trapped beneath it.

She tried to swim upward, but the downdraft of the boat had already begun to pull her down with it. She couldn't go up, even though she fought for it with all of her might.

Then in the distance, through the murky water she could see an opening in the cliff wall. A grotto. It was so low, there at the ocean floor, that she could have only seen it if she had been pushed into the water like this.

Immediately she knew that Charlotte had been right. They had found the forgotten cove that the poem in the pocket watch had been talking about. And because the boat was pulling her down, she decided that the grotto was a good place to swim for. And anyway, she might as well look for the silver pearl while she was here. She didn't think she would ever want to come to this treacherous place again.

So Grace stopped trying to swim upwards and instead she swam for the grotto with all of the determination that she could pull together. The opening was round and it glowed ever so dimly. The downdraft still pulled at her, but swimming away was easier than fighting it.

Grace knew that she was running out of air. She could feel herself beginning to grow faint. Her vision began blurring in and out, but she didn't stop; she couldn't stop.

The water's surface was now too far above for her to even imagine reaching it before she ran out of breath, but the grotto was right there. She reached the entrance and pulled herself through. The water inside the grotto was peaceful, as it was protected from the waves outside.

Grace could feel her lungs longing to expand; she was beginning to struggle for breath.

Inside the grotto, a shaft went directly up, where Grace could see light above. She pushed off from the ocean floor, shooting up now, towards the surface.

Suddenly she knew she wasn't going to make it in time. Her breath was nearly gone. But she swam with all that she had. She swam for her own breath... for Clarenne... for Edward... and she swam for Sam. But it wasn't enough. It just wasn't enough.

Looking up, she could see the light. It was as if she was dissolving into the light, everything thinning around her, the light growing. Encompassing. Consuming her. Time fell away - standing still for a moment. She stretched her arms out in front of her. She couldn't swim any longer. She couldn't move. She needed air to survive. But there was none.

She could feel her mind leaving. She was fading into the light above her...

So close. But just out of reach.

Her last thoughts were, "I love you, Sam! Think of me as the past gives you pleasure. Only think of our happiness..."

She hoped that he would remember her as Lottie would have wanted to be remembered.

Not how Clarenne and Edward had remembered her: as a mistake... something that was lost because of their own bad decisions - but as she *wanted* to be remembered. With fondness. Like light.

It was then, as these final thoughts flashed through her mind, that a sudden surge seemed to come from beneath her. An updraft. With unexplained force it pushed her upwards. It was almost as if some unseen force had given her a hard shove.

Something wanted her to live.

Grace lurched forward, suddenly breaking out of the water above the surface. She gasped for air, and was immediately revived. There was a ledge that she grabbed a hold of.

For a moment she just waited there, trying to comprehend what had just happened. And she cried. She cried that she was alive – even though it had seemed like it was her time to go. Even though her life had flashed before her eyes... she was alive!

And this told her more strongly than anything had ever told her before that she had a reason to be alive. She had something to do before she died.

Finally getting control of herself again, Grace looked before her. There was a shelf above the water, carved out of the white stone. There were steps beyond it. Grace pulled herself out of the water and up onto the ledge. There were three steps that led up to a pedestal. And there, sitting on the pedestal was a golden clamshell.

Grace hurried forward and picked it up with trembling hands. The golden clamshell was completely unharmed – in perfect condition, like it had been safe here for hundreds of years.

Carefully, she pried open the golden shell. Grace gasped when she saw that inside was the pearl, the silver pearl that Charlotte had lost her life trying to find. Grace had found the silver pearl.

There wasn't a lot of light in the cove, just the light that came from above and reflected off of the white, stone walls. And yet even here in this dim light, the pearl sparkled like a star.

Grace closed the golden clamshell with the pearl still inside. There was a thick chain that was attached to the golden shell. Grace slid this over her head, and she slipped the shell safely underneath her wet shirt.

And now, she thought of Sam... her heart pounded as she realized he would still be looking for her. He might even think her dead.

Her heart skipped a beat. She knew Sam. He wasn't one to give up. Not after all she meant to him.

Immediately, Grace turned away from the pedestal and hurried back down the steps.

She dove into the water, swimming for the floor and the entrance into the main cove.

The force from her dive carried her deeper and deeper into the water, but she still had to swim in order to get down deep enough. Once she got there, she turned and swam back through the opening again. As she left the protected cove, she felt herself wrapped in the fury of the stormy ocean again... hoping... praying that it wasn't already too late.

Fading Away

Sam pounded at the window several more times, still believing that he had seen Grace trapped inside the deck, when, in fact, it had only been a mirage.

Now his energy was failing him. He pounded once more and then fell forward with no more energy to spend.

With Grace gone, he felt there was little reason left to live. The last lingering hope in his heart had burned out and had completely given way to despair.

Sam fell forward, the last of his breath fading away.

...

Grace could see Sam now, and she watched as he fell forward. His head hit against the side of the boat, and she knew that he was unconscious.

She wanted to scream his name and yell for help, but being underwater she couldn't do anything. It was as if she was in the middle of a huge empty room – trapped. There wasn't anything she could do. She knew she wasn't strong enough to pull him up to the surface. Already, every muscle ached from her earlier exertions. Her own breath was again failing her, and there was no way she could possibly get him to the safety of the cave.

...

Though Edward didn't know the girl, he cried with Clarenne over her death, for it seemed again that the one he loved dearly was lost. But then with a jolt of fear, Edward watched earnestly, realizing that Sam hadn't appeared above the water for a while.

"Where is that boy?" he said anxiously.

"What?" Clarenne asked. "Sam is gone, too?"

"I have to go in after him," Edward said.

"You can't! You know your leg is broken," Clarenne reminded him.

"But I can't leave him there!" Edward raised his voice in frustration.

The water was already rising higher; it was coming up around their necks where they sat. Soon Clarenne knew they would have to move to higher ground in the cave... And after that, Clarenne knew, even though she didn't want to face the fact, that they were all going to die.

With the water level rising and the boat gone, they were stranded in this cave. And soon the cave would be filled with water, and they would be doomed to the same fate, which it seemed had already claimed Sam and Grace...

But though everything seemed like such a horrible ending, Clarenne felt a sense of happiness inside. For in her mind, everyone dying together was far more a happy ending than a few people dying and a few being left to live alone.

Edward was here, her good friend again, and she felt happier than she had felt for a long, long time. She wished it didn't have to end here, not now, not like this. She wished it could have gone on for the years that she had left to live. But she was already old, and how long would those years have lasted anyway?

It was all over...

...

Grace hung there, in the water for a moment, watching Sam's limp figure drifting in the water. She knew they didn't come out here to drown. That wasn't their purpose. Even though they were so many feet beneath the surface, and even though it seemed there was no hope left, and even though they were surrounded by darkness, Grace knew the darkness would turn to light if they could just see each other again.

She knew that having Sam there with her would somehow make everything all right.

Grace swam over beside him; she carefully touched his face, feeling a pulse in his chin. He wasn't gone yet, though she knew he would be if he didn't get air soon. His face was white, and he'd never seemed so lifeless to her before. She wished for light, for something to happen that would suddenly wake him. She pulled him to her and hugged him close, even though he didn't move at all.

But then as if by magic, the water above her began to glow. The rays of light shimmered down through the darkened water. Grace didn't know what it was, but the light gave her hope. It was as if the sun had suddenly come out in the middle of the stormy night, but that was impossible.

Pulling his arm over her shoulder, Grace knew she had to get Sam to the surface. He was much heavier than she had the strength to pull. It was a fool's hope to think she could do it, but she tried anyway. She pushed off from the ocean floor, and then again from the ship wreckage. The surface was getting closer now. She could see the light glowing brighter as she came closer and closer.

It was as if the lighthouse had come and found her. It had come and given her light when she was lost at sea, and somehow she knew that she could make it. Though odds were against her, the adrenalin within her upon seeing this light, gave her strength that she had never had before. And soon, she had broken through to the surface and she gasped for air.

For a moment she was above the water; she caught a glimpse of a large, massive shape in front of her. It was another boat! She couldn't understand how a boat could have found its way here. It didn't make any sense, but the boat was here, now.

Grace couldn't stay above the water for long. Treading water with both her and Sam's weight was nearly impossible.

Grace pulled herself back above the water for another breath, but this time she swallowed water as well. Coughing and choking, she lost more air. She was feeling faint, and her muscles cramped in their need for oxygen. She was losing her grip on Sam's arm.

Then they both slid beneath the water again. Though the safety of the boat was so close, it seemed like this was the end... it was all over.

But no, through the ripples and the light, Grace could see the silhouette of a lifesaver as it was hurled out into the water. Its shadows shimmered down through the ripples of the water, bending the light.

"One more time," she told herself.

And with the last of everything she had inside of her and a little bit more than she'd ever had before, she reached for the lifesaver.

And then it was there. It was there in her arm and she held onto it with all she was worth. It was a moment that made her tears flow. She had life in one hand, and the one she loved in the other.

The lifesaver was pulled in, and soon she was on the dock of the boat. She was out of the water, out of the dark. She was saved, and Sam was there, too.

HARD TO STARBOARD

Clarenne was suddenly next to Grace, "I thought I had lost you my sweet! Don't you ever scare me like that again!" She threw a blanket around Grace's wet shoulders.

Grace had too many questions to listen yet. "Where did this boat come from?" she demanded.

Grey stepped forward, "When you stole my boat, I figured I had better follow you."

"Grey!" Grace stood and hurried forward, throwing her arms around him.

Grey laughed, patting her softly on the back. "Everything is all right now. You were uncommonly brave, child."

But inside Grace knew that she hadn't done it alone. She knew that there had been that unseen force helping her. And instantly, like a shiver that ran through her, she knew who it was – it was Charlotte.

Charlotte had been with her the whole time. And when she had lost all hope, and wanted to give up... Charlotte had pushed her on. The real hero was Lottie – dear, sweet Lottie.

Unexpectedly, Sam started coughing and sat up. "Where am I?" he asked in confusion.

Grace rushed to his side and hugged him. "Sam!" she cried.

"Did I die?" Sam asked.

"No... Grey brought a boat and he rescued us," Grace explained.

"But you – you were trapped inside of the boat..." Sam stuttered, trying to make sense of what had happened.

Grace laughed, "No, I was never trapped inside of the boat." Her eyes sparkled with untold secrets. She sent a message through her eyes to Sam that said, "I've got news that I'll tell you later."

Sam smiled, understanding without any spoken words.

"Hard to starboard, Captain Grey," Edward said. "Just like the good ol' days."

"Just like the good ol' days," Grey repeated and he turned the boat out of the cove.

"I think my secret fishing hole has seen the last of its days," Edward said. "Besides, it's not secret anymore."

...

Grace could hardly believe how abruptly everything had changed and become all right. She had expected everything to end in a horrible fate – but it had all changed in a matter of seconds.

And as Grey's boat left the cove and entered the open sea, Grace realized that the sky had cleared, and there were stars above. The sky was filled with them, and like jewels of the night, they sparkled so brightly.

"Look, Sam," she said pointing at the sky.

They stood at the end of the boat, both staring out into the infinite sky. The stars filled the sky all the way down to the glow on the horizon. A full moon shone above them. And for a moment they just stood there staring.

Without warning, a shooting star fell halfway across the sky.

"Did you see that?" Sam whispered in awe.

"Yes, I saw it," Grace whispered back. "It was from Charlotte..."

Now that they were alone at the end of the boat, Sam thought it was a good time for Grace to explain what had happened.

"So, where were you? I couldn't find you any-where?" he questioned. "I was sure you had gone down in the boat."

"Well, in the diary Charlotte explained that Edward thought that the pearl was hidden somewhere around his secret fishing hole. When the boat cap-sized and I fell under the water, I got away into a cove..."

"The forgotten cove – you found it?" Sam raised his voice in his excitement.

"Sh!" Grace cautioned. "It was all of the way un-derwater! But I found it... and I found this..." Grace proudly pulled out the golden shell, which had been safely tucked inside her shirt.

Sam took it carefully in his hands and opened it. Now the pearl shone even brighter in the moonlight.

"You found the silver pearl!" Sam exulted, raising his voice again.

"Shh!" Grace warned, putting a finger to his lips. "Not so loud."

"So you were treasure hunting while I was trying to rescue you?" Sam teased.

Grace shrugged. "I guess you could say it that way..."

Sam laughed. "I don't believe you."

"Well I don't believe you either. You were the one who jumped out into the water and swam to that cave – you freaked me out."

"Well that was because I knew my uncle was still alive – I just knew it!" Sam insisted.

A sly smile crept across Grace's face. "And how did you know?" she pressed.

Sam understood her tease and laughed with her, "I guess it was just a gut feeling."

"You know," Grace said. "Sometimes following those comes in pretty handy."

"I guess I agree with you now," Sam said, handing the shell with the pearl back to Grace.

For a moment they just stood there, staring up at the sky again and feeling the gentle breeze. It was amazing to Grace how fast the night had changed from being a raging nightmare, to something completely blissful.

"Sam, I want you to take this back..." Grace held out the pocket-watch to Sam. "I think you were meant to have it. Think of it as a gift from Charlotte."

Sam took the pocket-watch carefully. "You know," he said. "My green composition book deserves to have our new findings logged in it."

"Alright," Grace laughed. "Whatever, you treasure hunter."

The shore was coming fast now, and they stared out into the distance... at the wide expanse of ever-changing water, the ocean that held memories... Charlotte had understood. It was so full of mysteries and secrets; one could never learn them all. It was a connection between what was past and what was now.

The ocean – it connects us all...

THE LIGHT OF THE LIGHTHOUSE

Back in the lighthouse, after they had all changed out of their cold, wet clothes and had warmed up again, they had dinner together.

Edward and Sam hadn't eaten such wonderful food from the kitchen in the lighthouse for a long, long time. Clarenne cooked it, and she truly knew how to cook. But really, any food was good to Sam, Grace, and especially to Edward. It was all very delicious.

Once the food had been put away, Grace and Sam took Clarenne on the treasure hunt that Lottie had left behind. First they had to put everything back in its rightful place so that Clarenne could find all the clues herself, though they did help her whenever she got stuck on the clues.

"I say we hide all of the clues again and keep the diary and everything here in the lighthouse, so that other people can go on Charlotte's treasure hunt and find her journal for themselves," Clarenne said once she had been through the whole thing.

It truly was too fine a treasure hunt for it to only be done once. Grace imagined children, years from now, doing the same treasure hunt that she herself had discovered with Sam. But she thought it would be better if they built onto the treasure hunt – shouldn't it get better over time? She told her idea to Sam.

"What would we hide?" Sam asked Grace.

"Hmm…" Grace said pretending to be thinking. She already had an idea, but she wanted Sam to think of it, too. "It would be cool if it was a book, don't you think?"

"Are you talking about my green composition book?" Sam smiled wryly.

Grace laughed. "What else?"

Sam glared at her, but it was a pretend glare. Actually, he was honored by her suggestion to hide his book. It made him feel almost as if his book was a treasure itself, and best of all, that it was a treasure to Grace.

"Okay, we can do that… But first, I have to finish writing it," Sam accepted.

"I guess that means we've got some more treasure hunting to do…" Grace teased, a twinkle in her eyes.

"But not when it's stormy outside!" Sam added.

"Right," Grace laughed. "I have a diary I'm writing… When it's done we can hide it somewhere around here, too."

"I know where my notebook can be hidden," Sam said thoughtfully.

"Where?" Grace wondered.

Sam took Grace to his room and proudly showed her the little nook in his bookshelf. She had to admit that it was ingenious.

When they returned, Edward was re-hanging the portrait of Charlotte in its proper place above the mantel. "I don't know why I ever took it down," he told Clarenne.

Clarenne stood and helped him get the picture straight. Then they both stood back and looked at it. The picture looked so natural there on the wall, having returned at last to its original home.

"You know, it's amazing to me how much I can still feel Lottie here... after all these years she's still around," Clarenne said, staring at the picture as her eyes filled with tears. "And to think that I had shunned her for so long... I'd never known I could feel her close..." Then she laughed and wiped away her tears.

For a moment they all just looked at the portrait. There Lottie would stay – like a photograph inside their hearts. She had changed them all. Grace thought it was amazing how someone she had never really known could change her so much, and it made her realize how much she needed to do with the time she had. For at any moment, it could be gone.

"Well," Clarenne said at last. "I think it's time for Grace and I to go home. Today has been an adventure, one I will never forget." She smiled at Edward.

Grace followed her aunt through the lighthouse and out the front door to the car. Sam and his uncle stood there, looking on.

"Wait," Grace said. She turned and hurried back to Edward and held out Lottie's diary. "This needs to go back to the watch in the lighthouse. Sam knows where it goes... but you might want to take a look at it first..." she said, handing him Charlotte's diary.

Edward smiled, and Grace could see the playful sparkle in his eyes, the same one that Charlotte had written about in the diary.

Then Grace turned to Sam. "I'll see you tomorrow?" her question was almost a statement.

Sam nodded. "Tomorrow."

She hugged him quickly and then hurried back to the car and climbed in. With the window rolled down, she turned and waved as the car drove away.

The full moon over the ocean cast a beautiful reflection, big and bright. And as they drove down the road with treetop canopies overhead, Grace couldn't help but watch the moon through the drifting branches.

The summer air had arrived again. It was a pleasant breeze that brushed against her face. There wasn't much to say in the car between Grace and her aunt because they both understood each other perfectly. Their experience out in the cove had brought them together as only trials can.

...

Back in the lighthouse, Sam and his uncle climbed the stairs towards the watch of the lighthouse. His uncle had to use crutches in order to do this, so they went at a slow pace. After all, they weren't in any sort of a hurry anyway. It was a beautiful night, and they had to stop at the main gallery and just gaze out across the island and into the night. They had to stare at the moon over the ocean with the few lazy boats that were drifting upon it now.

"It's never looked so peaceful," Sam's uncle said.

"No," Sam agreed.

Somehow, in the course of everything that had happened during the past couple days, Sam and his uncle had grown very close. They had shared secrets that neither one had known about before, and they had gone on adventures together, which had changed everything.

At last Edward broke the silence, "Thank you, Sam, for coming out for me. It was very brave of you."

Sam smiled and his uncle ruffled his hair. "You're growing up on me," he said. "Before I know it, you're going to be the one running this place..." This time his uncle laughed.

"But you'll always be here, too – right?" Sam asked.

"As long as I can..." Edward said, staring off into the distance and looking back through memories. "And as long as you keep me in your heart; then I'll be here forever..."

Sam hugged his uncle.

...

Soon the lighthouse was lit, and its light spread across the island like a steady star, calling to all who were lost or wandering. It was there, shining brightly.

...

"Grace gave me this book," Sam said. "She says I should read it..."

Edward took the book and read the cover. Then he smiled as he realized it was Lottie's old copy of <u>Pride and Prejudice</u>. He gave it back to Sam without saying a word.

"It's so boring though, I don't know how I could ever get through it," Sam complained.

"Just keep reading..." his uncle said. "You'll understand it in the end... and then you'll love it."

Then he turned and went to his own room with Lottie's journal, Sam noticed, tucked under his arm.

Sam shrugged and went to his own room with <u>Pride and Prejudice</u>.

...

In her room, Grace sat on her bed, finishing the entry in her journal. There was a lot to write about so it was taking her a while. She had laughed and cried as she wrote down the account of her exciting and scary night. Finally she finished the last sentence and ended it with a period.

She closed the book and reached over to set the book and pen on the nightstand. But her pen didn't quite make it to the stand. It fell on the floor and rolled under the bed. Hanging over the end of the bed, she lifted the dust ruffle and peered underneath. The pen wasn't very far under the bed, and she grabbed it. But as she drew it out, something on the far side of the bed caught her attention.

There was a little box propped on a shelf on the front end of the bed. She went around and pulled it out. It had obviously been hidden away. The box wasn't very large, just big enough to fit in her hand, but it was strangely heavy.

Suddenly Grace remembered what Clarenne had said when she had first shown her the room, that this had been her sister's room. This was Charlotte's room!

Grace was getting excited all over again. Lottie knew how to leave secrets behind – it made Grace wonder what else was hidden around the house somewhere.

She carefully opened the box and dumped its contents out into her other hand.

It was a snow globe.

Grace shook it and watched it for a minute. The sparkles fell like snow around the figure in the middle – a lighthouse. In fact it was the Mackinac Lighthouse. On the bottom of the snow globe was a crank. Grace wound it and a song began to play. Grace recognized it as one of Chopin's pieces from Opus 27. No 2, *Nocturne in D-Flat Major* it was called.

The base of the lighthouse was shaped like waves of the ocean around the rock that the lighthouse was on, but on the front there was a space where these words had been etched:

While ye have the light,
Believe in the light,
That ye may be the children of light...

Grace couldn't help but smile when she saw the music box.

And this music box made her think of the music box from her parents, and the picture she had hidden away deep inside of her drawer.

"Think only of the past as its remembrance gives you pleasure..." Grace whispered to herself.

She took a deep breath and opened her drawer. She gently picked up the picture and retraced the lines of her parents' happy faces... and everything was okay. She hugged the picture and carried it with her to the window. She stepped out onto the balcony and gazed out into the distance.

She could see the lighthouse. It shone brightly where it stood afar off. It looked as magical as it had the night she had seen it first, when she had seen it from the ocean liner. It was standing there for her, promising that there was hope, and that life would go on. Her parents had always been like a lighthouse for her – they had always given her hope. When she had been afraid, they had given her peace. When she had been weak, they had helped her find strength.

But now Grace realized here, that she herself was like the lighthouse. Though she was small and insignificant in comparison to the brightness of the lighthouse, she had a light all her own that she needed to shine. And she needed to keep her light burning – always.

It was the light of hope, a light that told souls, wandering in the night, to keep trying. Because, though they couldn't see it while they were lost in the dark, there were still peaceful shores waiting.

And though years would pass, seasons would change, and waves crash – she would always keep her light burning, knowing that the light would remain far longer than any mortal life ever could...

Made in the USA
Monee, IL
07 April 2021

65082773R00152